On Chill

Previously in part 2

Krystal

7:00 pm

Once my consciousness came back to me, I was traveling down the road going sixty-five miles per hour in a thirty. The kids were in the backseat sleeping in their car seats, but I don't remember us getting in the car. The last thing I could remember was Leon and me arguing before I grabbed a knife. I instantly looked down at my clothes to see if I had blood on them, but I had unknowingly changed from earlier. There was however a tan bandage on my hand, but I don't remember wrapping that either. The realization I was coming to was terrifying the hell out of me and I was starting to think the worst.

With no money in my account, and not wanting many people in my business, I knew the one person to call in this situation was, Nick. I couldn't go back to that house because just thinking about it scared me.

I pulled into a Marriott just off the freeway and parked to dial Nick's number. No, I hadn't known him for long, but I knew he would help me if he could.

"Hey, what's up shorty?"

"Where are you?"

"At Tish's house about to shower. You good?"

"No, not at all. Me and my ex had a big fight and I left with my kids."

"Well, what can I do to help you?" He said before I could even ask.

"Just a little money to get a room. After a couple of days, I will figure something out."

"Nah, we're going to do better than that. Can I meet you somewhere?"

"Okay, I'll send you the address" I replied before we hung up the phone.

After about thirty minutes of me sitting there, he pulled into the parking lot. He parked his car and stepped out with a blunt hanging out of his mouth that he put out on the ground. I stepped out of the car and when he saw my face the expression on his went from content to ready to murder.

"What happened to your face, Krystal?"

"Me and my ex got into a fight. He stole all my money for his child support."

"And he hit you?"

"Yes, I was hitting him first, but he hit me back."

"That doesn't matter, he hit you and I'm going to whoop his ass." Nick pulled up the waist of his pants as if he was going to fight right now.

"It's okay, you don't have to do that."

"Says who? I'm going to hurt that nigga for touching you." He went back to get inside his car.

"I said you don't have to Nick!"

"And why not? You trying to protect that abusive ass nigga?"

"No Nick I'm not! I think he's already dead. I think I may have killed him!"

Tish

10:00

My nature was to forgive even when I felt betrayed in the worst way. I couldn't stay mad at someone I loved for too long because I knew life was short. Especially short with the unfortunate shit happening around me. Dixon was the second person I've known to be shot in the past month. Thank God she too survived just as Nick.

"Dixie, is it hot enough for you?" I asked as she ate a spoonful of my famous homemade soup. I came to the hospital to bring her food since I knew she didn't have anyone she could depend on in Dallas. I was prepared to hate Dixon and my daddy for the rest of my life, but it was something about seeing her on the ground bleeding out that changed my perspective on it all. Was Dixon out of line yes, but was I prepared to hate her forever, no.

"It's perfect Bestfriend. Thank you so much for helping me the past couple of weeks. I don't know where I would be without you and Keys."

"Girl, you know it's nothing."

"Stop saying that, Tish. You know it took everything in you to be there for me. I know you're still upset about that situation with your father and I'm still so sorry it ever happened."

"Nah, I'm good. I don't want to talk about it."

"But we really should."

"I said, I don't want to talk about it. Let's just move forward and move on. We can't change the past. We can only prepare for the future."

"You're right. I'm sorry, you're so right." She fondled with her fingers.

"Well Chill is outside so I'm about to go. I'll be back in the morning to bring you breakfast. Call me if you need anything." I leaned down to hug her. When I left her room, I walked out to Chill standing outside his car in an all-black sweatsuit with a red beanie on his head. He smiled when he saw me and melted my heart that quickly.

"You need something to eat?" He asked after driving off.

"No, I'm good. Has Nick called and said Noelle is hungry?"

"Nah, I haven't heard from him."

"What do you mean? Are you sure everything is good?" I hurried to reach for my phone.

"Tish they good. Here look at the camera and see for yourself." He gave me his phone. On the screen was Nick sitting on the couch watching Noelle play on a small basketball goal. They are forcing this whole future WNBA stuff on my baby who just likes to play with dolls.

"Whew, okay. I'm just paranoid because this is the first time, we haven't been with her since the kidnapping."

"Yeah. I know. But they are good. Trust me, her uncle Nick will protect her. I'm more than sure about that." He sounded quite confident in himself. I leaned towards him in the seat as I always did any time, we were together. He was my comfort zone, and my sanctuary all in one.

I wasn't paying attention to where we were going because I was deeply invested in my Facebook timeline. Two girls I went to high school with were arguing about their shared baby daddy and I thought it was funny. I'm glad I didn't have those problems.

Chill and I soon pulled up at a building that was not our place.

"Why are we here baby?"

"We meeting with my financial advisor. This building is a branch of his company."

"Oh, okay." I carelessly shrugged my shoulders as he pulled up to the valet.

We got out of the car, and I followed Chill up the elevator and to a conference room with windows that seemed to look over the entire city of Dallas. A short white man in a brown suit came into the room with a personality as loud as his yellow tie.

"Hello, welcome, welcome. Thank you for always being on time my guy." He gave Chill a firm handshake.

"William, this is Tish, Tish this is William." Chill introduced us to one another.

He offered us a seat at a very large table and the sheer size of the table made me a tad bit intimidated.

"Chill, what's this about?" I asked when my curiosity got the best of me.

"Don't worry, he will tell you in a second." He replied, sitting back in his chair.

"Okay, so we are here to discuss Mr. Malachi Saint's fortune and assets as far as the 2024 year. Mr. Saint your total net worth as far as today is 1.2 billion dollars. In such of your untimely death, your assets will be left to seventy-five percent Noelle Saint, and twenty-five percent to Nicolas Saint." He went on before Chill interrupted him.

"I want to go ahead and stop you right there. The paperwork does state that if anything happens to me Noelle can't touch the money until she is twenty-five correct?"

"Correct. We recommended the age of twenty-five because we find children are beginning to be financially responsible."

"Okay, and that's fine but I want to change something else. I want her Mother Tish Gage to take over the funds immediately in my demise. There is no need to make Noelle wait to access my money if I die before she comes to age." My bottom jaw dropped.

"What does that mean Chill?"

"It means if I die tomorrow or anytime in the next 23 years then you and Noelle will live a good life. Y'all both deserve that, and I trust you will do what's right."

"You trust me with a billion dollars?"

"I would trust you with 1.2 billion." He said with a smile.

"Anyway, I also want my daughters' direct assets to go down from seventy-five percent to sixty percent. I want fifteen to go to Tish. She deserves it for raising my daughter so damn perfectly."

"You got it, boss man. I can draw up all of the paperwork and we can get it signed in my New York office. Are there any more direct changes as of now?"

"None. We should be good." They conversed and I was honestly too shocked to speak. I wanted to be happy but getting that money would mean Chill wasn't in my life anymore. I would rather life just as it is with him in it because he's worth way more than a billion dollars.

After we left the office building Chill took me home because he had to catch a flight out of town. He left us in the care of Nick but to be honest, I just wasn't scared anymore.

When I came into the house I heard Noelle giggling down the hall, but I didn't go bother her just yet because I wanted to go take a peaceful shower first. I tiptoed into the restroom and turned my shower on along with the faucet in the tub.

My phone started ringing just as I thought about Chill, but it was actually my dad calling who I forwarded to voicemail. When I did that, he instantly texted me,

This is life or death, please call me back.

I'm not sure if my daddy was pulling my leg or not but when I read his message, I had to call. The phone rang only two times and then he picked up the phone clearing his throat.

"Hello."

"What is going on Dad?"

"Nothing as of now. I just wanted to hear your voice. Tell you I love you before I go away for good." I sat silently because I was trying my hardest not to be rude.

"Tish, you know I love you right? You know you and your sister are my moon and stars. Without you both I wouldn't be the man I am today. You know what losing your mother did to my heart. It made me weak. It made me fragile. It made me look for love in all the wrong places."

"Dad, I'm about to get in the tub. Can this wait?"

"Unfortunately, it can't baby girl. I won't have the chance to tell you this again." His word choices got my attention.

"Why are you talking like that? I'm mad at you now, but I never said it would be forever. I'm just disappointed more than anything. I thought you were perfect."

"And it pains me that your perception of me has changed since you found out about my mistakes. Listen I deeply apologize for involving myself with your friend. To be honest I wasn't thinking about you when I fell in love with her. I was looking at her deep brown skin, her almond eyes, and her full pink lips all things your mother had."

"So, you think that's supposed to make me feel better about you two sneaking around? Because she reminded you of my mother?"

"No, no, I didn't say that because I know it won't. Just like I know nothing will truly ever make me happy again. With the loss of your mother, the loss of someone I was beginning to love, and the loss of my daughter's respect. I just can't go on anymore."

"Daddy, stop talking like that."

"I'm sorry baby but it's true. I just wanted to call you and tell you I love you one last time."

"Daddy."

"I love Noelle."

"Dad!"

"And I love my baby girl Tasha with everything in me. I want you to take care of her okay? I love you, goodbye my girl."

The phone disconnected, my heart started to race, and my hands were shaking. God, please don't let this be happening right now. I don't think my heart can take it.

Chill

Me and Keys got on a private jet to go to California, and I was happy to have my right-hand man on my side again. Me and this nigga have been through so much and accomplished so much shit together. I wouldn't be as rich without him, and he could get the world from me. I don't think he even knew how much I cut for him and that's the truth.

"So what's good man? What's been going on in married life?" We sat across from each other in the spacious G6 jetliner.

"Shit, it's going. Where I don't know, but it's going." He leaned forward and shook his head. I picked up that quickly he had a lot on his mind. I've known Keys for a long time. He's never been able to hide his emotions unlike me.

"Talk to me bruh, what's going on in your head?"

"Man, just a lot. I can't believe shit went down the way it has. I might've done something that I shouldn't have. Now I feel guilty as fuck to be honest."

Guilt, Keys, that didn't even sound right in the same sentence. I sat up in my seat and put out my cigar. The flight attendant came up with two glasses of bourbon straight and I waited until she went back in the back to respond.

"Don't talk in riddles bruh, tell me what you did. You know wrong or right I'm on your side."

"I know, I just." He took a deep breath as I sat hanging on his words.

"Bruh, you know Dixon just got shot outside your place, right?"

I nodded my head yes.

"Well, I did that. I paid someone to shoot her."

"Someone like who? You gave a hitman my family's address when you know what we just went through?" I tore my face up as my eyes widened in disbelief.

"No, no, I didn't tell niggas it was your place. It was Snoopy's cousin Big Wet. I told him I was going to a meeting there. He doesn't know you are connected to that place at all."

I grabbed the cigar from the ashtray and lit it because I was trying to stay calm.

"I see you angry bruh and I apologize for it. I just feel like my back against the wall with her. I didn't know what else to do."

"Your back against the wall because y'all got married? Divorce the bitch and move on. What type of hold she got on you to need her killed?"

He simply shook his head and dropped it to the ground.

"Nothing really."

"Well, why try to kill the girl? It's plenty of niggas out here that deserve death over a female you fuckin. Shit why you didn't kill Stella?"

"Because she means a lot to my kids."

"Okay, and Dixon means a lot to my kid so that doesn't mean shit to you?"

"I didn't think about it like that. I was just trying to make my problems go away all at once. But she survived and now I'm asking myself if I did the right thing. Should I have just done it another way?"

"Well, I hope you know killing a female in downtown Dallas ain't the way to handle shit. Killing her in general because that is not an option. Tish and Noelle already been through too much and a nigga close to me ain't putting them through nothing else."

"I understand."

"Nah bruh I need you to feel me. Figure out something else. If you take a L in this situation financially then you just take a L."

I leaned back in my seat. This nigga Keys was buggin' trying to get Dixon killed. I'm glad the bitch survived.

When the plane landed in the airport there was a throw-away car with fake tags waiting for us here. My guy Jack had everything set up after driving here from Vegas. Keys and I hopped in the car and in the backseat we're all the guns I requested.

"My nigga, my nigga. If you ever fall off, then I know who number two going to be." I joked after grabbing the AR from under the seat. Keys got the old-school GPS machine and we put in the address of the nursing home.

"30 minutes away bro."

"Cool. Let's take off." I replied and Keys drove off. When we got to the nursing home, we parked in the back corner near the only entrance.

"I wonder what kind of car he driving." Keys said scoping out the scene.

"I bet it's something a nigga up fifty million would drive. This nigga is not used to shit. He lying low but he is still flashy and you can't do both." I kept my eyes on the streets. I only looked away when Tish texted me to call her when I got a chance. Just as I was about to, Keys spoke up getting my attention.

"Jaguar F-Pace, coming into the parking lot right now."

I quickly put my phone down.

"Alright, go, go, let's make a move on this nigga now." Keys whipped around the building to where Shadow was parking. We hopped out of the car before he could react, and I knocked the glass out his window with the bottom of my rifle. There was a quick lil struggle with him until I put my arm around his neck and choked his ass to sleep right in the front seat of his car.

When I dragged his bitch ass onto the ground, he was unconscious, and we both looked around to make sure no one was watching.

"You want to pop him, or you want me to do it." Keys pointed his gun to Shadow's unconscious body.

"Nah we not popping him right here. I got somewhere I want to take him for a little date. Here put these cuffs on him and help me get him in the trunk."

After putting him into the trunk I got in the driver's seat because I wanted to get to the warehouse as fast as possible. The feeling of having this nigga in my possession was one I couldn't explain. I never wanted to kill somebody so bad, but then again do it so slowly.

When we got to the warehouse Jack was sitting outside smoking a black and mild.

"Pretty rich niggas. What's up? Y'all got here quicker than I thought."

"You know we move like the feds when it's time. Help us get this big mutha fucka out."

When we opened the truck, Shadow's eyes were opened and wide like a scared child's. I made sure I didn't look away from him so he could see what was going to happen to him just by the fire in my eyes. I was hoping he woke up while in the trunk because I remember this nigga used to be claustrophobic as hell. Our friends used to make him pee on himself trapping him under covers.

"Go get me that tape out the back before this nigga starts screaming." I directed Keys and Shadow closed his eyes and began to chuckle.

"I knew this would happen." He opened his eyes now displaying a cocky smirk.

"Nigga shut the fuck up. As a matter of fact, don't. I want to hear your emotions getting the best of you as you realize you slowly dying. Talk your shit, say whatever you want because I want to hear it all. Now wait in the trunk for a minute, I need to smoke first." I closed him up again.

Keys handed me the duct tape, but I chunked it on the ground and pulled a blunt out of my pocket. I knew as angry as I was, I wouldn't move smart right now. I needed to calm down so that I could truly enjoy killing this nigga. I was on some demonic ass shit right now.

"So, you not going to use the tape on him? You know this nigga about to scream."

"Let him, I don't give a fuck. It will be music to my ears and we're in the middle of nowhere." I took long pulls from the blunt. Shadow could be heard squirming in the trunk, and I could hear in his voice he was starting to get scared.

"Aye!! Open this mutha fucka!"

"Shut the fuck up nigga. Why are you rushing death?" I yelled back to the trunk.

"Say, Chill, you might want to open up and listen to what I got to say. I can tell you who helped me get to you! Just open the trunk!" Shadow screamed, and we all looked at one another.

"Man, ignore this nigga. He just wants to get out."

"Nah, let me see what he talking about. I want to murder who helped him too." I hit the unlock button on the trunk ready to hear the name of who I needed to find next.

Chapter 1

Chill

10:30 pm

When I opened the trunk, shadow started to speak but was instantly stopped when a hail of bullets started firing into his body.

Pop, pop, pop, pop.

I looked to my left and Keys had his gun in his hand.

"Why the fuck did you do that?" I pushed him back towards a brick wall, pinning him at his neck. He out of everybody should've known I liked to swing my sword in an execution. It was the only way I felt better after someone wronged me.

"My bad bruh. My emotions just got the best of me!"

"Your emotions nigga? What about mine? You know I had a plan for this nigga and you just fucked it up!"

I punched him in the center of his stomach making him curl over. My nostrils flared as I looked down on him wondering why the fuck, I hadn't killed him yet. I kept punching his ass until I felt like stopping and this nigga knew better than to fight back. These licks would for sho feel better than bullets.

"I said my bad bruh, damn! I care about your family too and I hate this nigga just as much as you. I lost control of myself. You don't understand that?"

"No, you don't understand! You killed him and now we will never know who else deserves to die right along with him!" I punched him again sending his ass to the ground. I didn't give a fuck about his weak ass heart right now.

Jack walked over towards us and cautiously grabbed me by my arm.

"Boss man don't take it too hard on him. I'm sure that nigga Shadow was lying anyway. I'm sure he got his info from following us around for we don't know how long. Him saying that was just a ploy to get you to open the truck." Jack tried to be the voice of reason. I know he was probably right but that still didn't mean I didn't want to torture this nigga. Now all I could do was burn his body and watch him turn into a crisp.

"Y'all take this nigga out the trunk and get rid of him." I gave them orders making them move like their feet were on fire. I walked around to the driver's side of the car and sat in the seat as they unloaded Shadow's body. When my phone rang from the glove compartment, I wasn't going to answer it until I saw Tish was calling.

"What up mama? Can I call you back on the plane?"

"No, Chill my daddy is dead! He's gone, he's gone!" She cried into the phone.

"Huh, what happened?"

"He jumped off a building near our place!"

"Damn, what the fuck? When did this happen?"

"I don't know Chill. Just tell me why because I don't get this! I don't know how I'm going to tell my sister. She is not going to take this well. Why God!" She let out a scream that put more hurt in my heart than I think I'd ever felt.

"Tish listen, I'm coming back. Give me a few hours and I'll be there, okay."

I assured her as she wept like a child. I can't believe Winston would do some shit like this to my family. They didn't deserve any more pain, now here it was again at their doorstep.

Chapter 2

Nick

11:15 pm

After I put Krystal and her kids in a hotel room, I left to go check out the scene at her house. I didn't know what I was going to find there since Krystal didn't have memory of what happened. I mean I get it; I blacked out all the time too when I got mad. I once almost killed a dude while fighting him during a mental blackout. When I came to, the dude had a fractured rib, and I was already in handcuffs on my way to jail.

Krystal better know I cut for her doing this shit because the average man wouldn't. But that's just the thing, I'm not your average man. I now knew what it feels like to take a life and I wasn't scared to do it again.

When I pulled into their driveway, I cut the car off and instantly noticed all the lights were still on in the house. Once I stepped out, I crept up to the door and twisted the knob going straight into the house. I grabbed my gun from my waistband and moved quietly through the rooms. It was cold as ice for some reason and the entire house smelled good like Krystal's clothing. I noticed she had decorations everywhere and pictures up on every wall. Krystal seemed like a great mother and wife besides her infidelities with me. I can't fault her for that though. Her husband pushed her right into my arms.

When I stumbled into the kitchen, I heard a moaning sound coming from the other side of the center island. I walked around and spotted Krystal's husband lying on the ground, bleeding out from several places. Krystal really did go crazy on this nigga I see.

"Please help me?" He pleaded desperately as I squatted down beside him. He was breathing heavily and reaching out for me like I was a paramedic or some shit.

"Please call 911. My wife stabbed me with a butcher's knife. I've lost a lot of blood, and I can't move."

"Damn bro, that sucks. What did you do to make her that mad?" I rubbed in my chin hairs while looking over his body. When our eyes finally met, his pupils started to dilate, and I couldn't tell if he was dying or having a revelation about something.

"Hold on. Aren't you the guy who came to my house looking for a date or something? What are you doing in my house?" I smiled and laughed a little because his fear was funny as fuck.

"I'm not here to answer any of your questions my boy. Just know my name is Nick, and I'm the one who's been knocking your wife's walls down."

"What do you mean?"

"You heard me."

"Man get the fuck out of my house! Why the fuck did you come here?"

"I thought you wanted my help."

"Forget your help. Get the fuck out of here!" He struggled to yell.

"Damn, you really are an ignorant mutha fucka I see. I should've known though. No man with common sense would put their hands on a female as pretty as Krystal. When I see her, all I ever want to do is eat that lil fat pussy and make her grab my ears."

"Lil nigga, I said get the fuck out of my house! I don't know why you are here! Leave!"

My phone started to ring from my pocket, but I ignored it. I was tending to something more important right now.

"Listen Leon. I'm here to put you out of your misery so you won't be suffering any longer. I'm sure you've been lying here hurting for a while. It's the least I could do." I replied, standing over him. I pulled my gun from my waistband and screwed the silencer on.

"No, bro. Please, I have kids." He held his arms up towards the gun.

"I know you have kids' nigga, but I don't give a fuck. Rest in piss Ike Turner."

I pulled the trigger and shot him three times in his chest. The smell of gunpowder filled my nose, and I felt just as powerful as I did when I shot that nigga in his back with Chill. The only thing that broke my gaze from his dead body was a call coming through my phone from Tasha.

"What up, beautiful?" I answered after stepping over Leon.

"Hey boo, where are you? I feel like having some of you in my guts." I chuckled at her bluntness and then looked down at Leon's body.

"I'm cleaning up right now, but I'll be by there as soon as I'm done."

"See if you lived with me, you wouldn't be cleaning up shit. I would treat you like a king just for sex."

"And I know you would. I'll be by there in a couple of hours."

"Okay."

I replied, then heard hard knocks through her phone.

"Damn, someone's beating at my door. Let me answer it, but I'll see you soon."

"Okay," I replied and she hung up the phone.

While Leon's dead body was on the floor, I started moving about the kitchen to get rid of all the blood and evidence. Good thing Krystal had a bunch of cleaning products that I could use. I would've torched the place, but they would find the body and still figure out the cause of death. I wanted this bitch ass nigga's body to disappear forever, so no one had to explain anything that happened to him.

After cleaning up all the blood, I went into the garage to attempt to find something to drag him out with. Inside, I found two large car covers and two cement blocks on the back of a basketball goal. I opened the garage and backed my car inside so that I could load him up. I lined one of the car covers on the inside of the trunk and then dragged him out to the garage on the other one.

It took me about an hour and a half to get done with the place but I'm sure I left the kitchen spotless. There were no traces of a murder anywhere in there and if there was, it would take the best crime lab to find it. I left their house and called Krystal to calm her nerves since I knew she was waiting to hear from me.

"Was he there? Did you find him?" She asked, as soon as she picked up the phone.

"He was there, but I saw him getting in the car with some girl. He had a suitcase with him."

She exhaled deeply, relieved after my lie.

"Thank God. I hope he stays gone and never comes back."

"Yeah, I'm sure he will. But I'll call you back when I get home. I have to stop at the store."

"Okay, thank you for everything you did tonight. You're truly a lifesaver."

"You're welcome, but it's the least I could do. You saved my life remember." I replied, and she giggled as I pulled out of her driveway.

I drove to a desolate bridge I saw on a map that was over a large body of water. There were no cars or houses in sight, so I knew this was a good spot. I had his body chained up to the bricks I found at his house so he wouldn't float up. I've never done any shit like this before, but I've listened to my brother and his crew talk enough to know the ins and outs of getting away with murder. I wish I could get his ass to the crematorium to burn him up, but this would have to do.

After I left the dump site, I turned my phone back on once I was close to Tish' and Chill's penthouse. Instantly, my line started to ring, and it was a call from my brother which I always answered.

"Yo, what's up mysterious ass nigga?"

"Nigga, where you been at? I need you to go to Tasha's apartment now and check on them. Their daddy just killed himself."

"Damn, for real!"

That news genuinely shocked the fuck out of me because of who it was. I mean I didn't know the nigga well, but Tasha talked about her daddy all the time.

"Yeah, shit crazy so get over there now."

"Alright bruh, I'm on my way," I replied, hanging up the phone. It's crazy how empathy works because I feel worse about that nigga killing himself than I did about killing another man tonight.

At least I feel like Leon deserved to die. He was a fuck ass nigga who did fuck ass shit and the world would be a much better place without him.

Chapter 3

Dixon

3 months later

7:30 am

When I opened my eyes, I got up from my bed and went to the front door to pull the trash can inside. We had valet trash pick up in my apartment complex and a hefty $100 fine if we left it out past 7:00 am. Money wasn't an issue right now, but avoiding fees was still a force of habit. Me and my man had to be rich forever so wasting money wasn't an option.

We've been staying at my apartment, booed up like a true newlywed couple. We both had issues going on in our lives which bonded us together even more. Getting to know him made me like him even more than the physical attraction. I've fallen in love with this man and I'm sure he felt the same way about me.

Keys had been showing me so much affection and never failed to mention how much he appreciated me. He even made his mama respect me by checking her any time she said something negative about me. We watched movies together, went out to eat dinner, and most importantly fucked sunup to sundown.

Though everything in my relationship and personal life was going well, Tish and I still haven't spoken so that kind of put a damper on my happiness. The last time I heard from her she had written me months ago saying she would rather I not come to her father's funeral. I couldn't get upset about it because I honestly blamed myself for his suicide too. I mean, I know I didn't tell him to jump but I knew Winston was weak, and I led him on which pushed him over the edge. When I heard about his death, I cried for days because I couldn't believe what he did. That just shows you how powerful love actually is, and I never wanted to feel any heartbreak like that.

They had a small service for Winston which was live-streamed by the church because it couldn't hold many guests. He was buried in a white casket, and they couldn't show his body because of how mangled it was. I prayed for Tish and Tasha the entire length of the service because I was watching them take it hard. Shit, I still prayed for their strength to this day and prayed to get my friend back. Just as she forgave me the first time, I'm sure she could forgive me again. At least I hoped so. I could live without my relationship with Krystal's judgmental ass, but I needed Tish in my life. She was the type of friend everyone needed.

Not only were Tish and I distant, but Chill and Keys weren't speaking either. I'm sure it's not because Chill found out what Keys did since Keys was still breathing. When I would ask about their distance, he would say it's just business stuff and it's no big deal. Who knows if it was or not, but I wanted them to be back cool one day. Then maybe in the future, we could take a couple's trips together to islands we've never been to before.

"Dixon!" Keys called my name from the other room.

"What baby?"

"Come here! Hurry up!" He yelled, making me run to my bedroom. Ever since his first heart attack, I was so cautious about his health. He knew I didn't allow him to do anything at all that could risk him having another one. I even made him stop when we were fucking every fifteen seconds to catch a break when he was fucking me too fast. That nigga wasn't dying on top of me.

"Yes, what's wrong? You okay?" I asked when I burst into the room. He was laying on his back with his dick standing up and I folded my arms with an attitude.

"Really Keys, you scared me." I pouted watching him start to slowly stroke his dick.

"I'm sorry baby, but I missed you."

"Missed me? Keys we just woke up." I gave him attitude because my heart rate was still high.

"So, I wanted you in here with me. You know I'm hooked on you." He smiled, and I was left cheesing back at him.

"Your ass is so spoiled."

"And yo ass is so fine. Now take that shirt off and flaunt that sexy ass body for me." He grinned as he signaled for me to come over. As much as I wanted to maintain my attitude, I couldn't looking at his long chocolate dick in front of me.

I walked over to him as I undressed, and he sat on the side of the bed watching me. Once I was in his arms, he started caressing my body, kissing me all over my neck, my lips, and even over my gunshot wound which I was insecure about. Keys made me feel sexy, beyond just being confident. Even the things I didn't like about myself he hyped up. That's why I knew that nigga loved me.

Once I straddled him, he quickly took my breast into his mouth and sucked on them as if he were being breastfed. I liked it, but I liked pleasing him more, so I attempted to get on my knees before he stopped me.

"Don't forget we got that flight in a couple of hours. Just get on top so we can go." He reminded me of something I honestly forgot about.

"Oh yeah, but you know I don't like getting on top anymore. Come on, hit it from the back."

"Nah, I want you to ride this mutha fucka."

"No, Keys."

"No? Why are you always so scared."

"You know why. I get on your dick and lose my mind. I don't know how to stop." Keys started to laugh.

"Dixon, that's not the reason I had that heart attack so stop blaming yourself. It was my heart and all the liquor and drugs I was doing. It was bound to happen anyway." He tried to downplay my fear.

"You saying that but you don't know. I'm the nurse remember."

"I know, but that's the good thing about it all. I know you're going to save your man." He flipped his hair over his shoulder.

"Now come to daddy and ride this dick. You know you want to."

I rolled my eyes with a smirk on my face. This nigga always gets what he wants with me.

Keys laid back on the bed and I climbed over his dick before slowly sliding it in between my already wet pussy lips. I rocked back and forth a minute before I got off my knees and got into a crabwalk position to bounce on him that way. My thighs were burning, but my pussy felt so good it didn't matter.

"Fuck, this pussy so good." He mumbled under his breath.

"You like that daddy?"

"Yeah, I like that. Fuck just like that." He encouraged me while moaning so sexily. Keys grabbed my ankles, squeezing them so tightly I knew he was about to nut. Just hearing his breathing and subtle grunts also made me climax so hard.

"Fuck!" I screamed and just like a chain reaction Keys put even more cream in between my legs. After we both came, he kissed me so hungrily, dragging his teeth against my bottom lip.

"Now let's get ready for this flight. I can't miss it. It's important." he tapped me on my ass twice and I got up getting straight to what he told me to do.

After he and I had sex, we both took a shower and started to pack for the airport. Since Chill and Keys weren't talking, the private jet luxury was gone for the moment. We had to go through the airport like regular broke-ass people and I hated that.

At around noon we called for an Uber which came and dropped us off at terminal A. Going through the airport, I felt like I was in hell since it had been a while. I realized now that Keys needed more money than he had because I wanted private jet luxuries too. We shouldn't have to lower our standards because Chill isn't around.

Keys problem was he was comfortable being the sidekick to a billionaire instead of trying to be one himself. I had a few investment ideas I was going to pitch to him one day, so we could double our money. One was asking him to buy a few houses to renovate and sell. That would make us more income and I could also give a house to my mother. It would solve a whole lot of my problems all at once.

When we sat at the terminal, it was announced that our flight was delayed by an hour. Both anxious and irritated we decided to eat at the Pappasitos restaurant in the airport. We sat down at a booth waiting to order our food when Hippo Hellen, called with her nagging us. I couldn't stand his mama.

"Alright mama I understand that, but Cassie needs to learn to save her money better. This is the third time this month she is in a bind."

I was eavesdropping and rolling my eyes because I knew what kind of call this was. His leeching ass family was another reason why he would never be filthy rich like Chill. Giving them handouts every week was draining his pockets.

Once he hung up the phone, he took an aggressive bite from the bread at the table. His hands were bald up and his face looked like he wanted to kill someone.

"Baby, why do you let your family worry you like that?"

"Because they're family. What else am I supposed to do?"

"I don't know, maybe not bail them out any time they ask. Sometimes rock bottom is where people have to land to get it together."

"That's easy for someone with no family to say." He dropped the bread he was eating and sat back in his seat.

"Damn, okay."

"I mean no offense, but you don't have people that need you like me. The only family I ever here you talk about is your mama, which you've sent her cash in jail since we've been together. Is that letting her hit rock bottom?"

"Okay Keys, I get it. Calm down." I dropped my bread too because I was no longer hungry.

"I'm sorry Dix, they just got me stressed."

"I know, which is the only reason I said anything. You shouldn't be stressed period. Not even over people you love. Trust me Keys, I have family that I used to deal with in the past, but they sucked me dry. I chose peace over blood and haven't regretted it one day. You will see how easy life gets once you let that need to help go. I promise you." I finished, and he just nodded his head in agreement.

He was hard on the outside, but I know once I break through that exterior, he would be putty at my fingertips.

"You probably right but it's easier said than done. My mama and my sisters mean a lot to me."

"I know they do but helping them so much is hurting them in the long run. Leave them with no other options and watch them blossom." I reached over the table to grab his hand.

"I love you Keys."

"I know. I appreciate you." He replied. Though I didn't get an I love you, I knew it was coming one day.

"Delta flight 567 now boarding at gate 23." We heard and went towards the gate with our early boarding passes.

When we landed in Vegas Keys said he had business to handle and a package to pick up as soon as we got there. He had me book a hotel room for only a few days because he said he wanted to return to Dallas this week.

Once we got off the plane, he grabbed our bags and we Ubered to the Chill's place where Keys had his car parked. I thought we would be going to the hotel room once we got the car, but we instead pulled up to some random building off The Strip. When Keys took off his seat belt I did too, ready to get out with him. I'd learned quickly over time that Keys liked me at his side for safety purposes.

When I opened the door, Keys stopped me in my tracks.

"You don't have to go, just stay here and let me go handle this. I'll be back out soon."

"You sure babe?"

"Yeah, you good here. Just lock up."

"Okay," I replied before he closed the car door. I reached into the backseat and grabbed my backpack to get the self-help book that I was reading in my downtime. Getting lost in the pages, I was unaware of how long Keys had been gone but it seemed like no time had gone by before he was knocking on the back door. I unlocked it, never lifting my head from the book. It wasn't until I heard a child's voice that I looked behind me.

"Daddy, are we going to see Mama?" said a little girl with braids and beads in her hair. There were also two little boys with him that looked like twins with him. As a matter of fact, these were the same kids that Stella brought to the hospital the day Keys had a heart attack. That meant these were his fuckin kids.

"Baby I didn't know we were getting your kids while we are down here. We could've gone and got them some toys or something to play with."

"Nah, no toys. We don't need anything extra on the plane ride home." Keys shook his head as if he was stressing hard.

"What do you mean the plane ride home?"

"It means they are coming back to Dallas with us. This is the CPS building Dixon. They got taken from Stella's grandma because my son took weed to school last week."

"What the fuck?"

"Yeah, it's a fucking shame I know." He helped them into the car.

I didn't say anything else because I didn't know what to say without sounding rude. All I know is I didn't want any kids in my life right now, especially not kids of the woman I hate. Them being with us was about to fuck up our whole vibe and I did not agree with this shit at all.

Chapter 4

Krystal

The next morning

9:00 am

Martha had me down at the police station yet again trying to locate Leon. I tried telling her that his snake ass probably ran off with his other family, but she didn't want to believe that. Because I didn't want my business out about Nick, I told her that I saw him leave with a female myself. That didn't work because they still wanted to believe something was wrong. She felt like she knew her son so well and there were certain things he just wouldn't do. Yeah fucking right.

Okay, yes, in the back of my mind, I wondered if he was okay and if I had done something bad that night. However, another part of me didn't care. I was just glad to have him out of my life.

"Sir, I understand he is an adult but it's not like my son to not call me. My birthday just past last week and he didn't reach out. That lets me know something is not right. I'm telling you; something is going on with my child." Martha started to get upset.

"Ma'am as we've told you time and time again, we're doing everything we can to locate your son. We will get to the bottom of this one day, but we can't promise it will be today. We have to work the case as evidence comes in and we don't have much to work with right now."

"Well, dammit get some more evidence! This is my child, not just some case! This is not law and damn order!" I grabbed her arms and walked her away from the counter.

"Calm down mama."

"No Krystal, there ain't no calm down."

"Yes, it is. We can't make them our enemies. I know you're worried, but we can't get arrested up here and we need them on our side. They may never look for him if we disrespect them too bad." Her frail body was shaking, and she rested her forehead on her fingertips.

"Lord Jesus give me strength."

She started to weep.

"I just miss my baby Krystal. He's, my baby boy and he's never not told his mama happy birthday."

"I know, that's so not like him. None of this is." I hugged her tightly.

"Come on, let's get you home in case he calls." I helped her out of the police station and to my car.

We left the police station but of course, I had to stop by her favorite store Family Dollar, to get things she needed. She was never too sad not to run her errands I'll tell you that. Martha loved The Family Dollar store like it was the mall.

I let her go in by herself because she took forever in a store. While she was in there I was going to sit back and grade these end-of-the-year tests I had sitting in my back seat. My students all complained about these questions being difficult which made me feel guilty about my teaching efforts for the year. Had my preoccupied mind interfered with that?

"Really Sydney. Now, this question was an easy one." I griped as I went down the front page. I was locked in scanning through the grades until I heard a laugh that sounded so familiar. I lifted my head, and it was Tasha walking past my car on the phone.

"I don't know if I can make it girl. We will see what Nick says but if he's not coming over then I'm down."

What Nick was she talking about? I cracked my car door and then shouted to get her attention.

"Hey, Tasha!"

"Girl, I didn't know that was you in here. What you doing on my side of town?"

"I was taking my mother and law to the police station around the corner."

"Still no good news?" She folded her bottom lip over. I hate I had to accept sympathy from people about Leon even though I didn't want any.

"Nope, not a word from him but I'm still keeping faith though."

"Yeah, you got to."

"Yeah, well anyways girl. Were you just talking to Tish? I was going to call her when I got home."

"Nah, I'm going over there later though. I was talking to my friend Cece, remember her?"

"Yeah, I remember her and her loudmouth." We both laughed together.

"I heard you say something about seeing a Nick. What Nick are you seeing? You and Tish doing that brothers dating sister's thing?" I tried to keep me being nosey as lighthearted as possible.

"Nah, I'm talking about another Nick. You don't know him." She waved it off, so I changed the subject.

"Oh, tell me something girl. Well, anyway, you look cute today. I hope you feel just as good as you look."

"Thanks, friend." She replied, smiling and batting her eyes.

With what she and Tish have been through I sympathized with them so much. I hope one day they both truly find happiness. I'm however positive that Tish has already found hers. Her and Chill were meant for each other and my new favorite couple.

"Yes, I feel so much weight lifted off me since the funeral."

"That's good. You know I'm there if you need me."

"You know I know that girl." She smirked, leaning into my window to hug me.

"Well let me go in this store so I can be on time to meet my plug at the Chevron station down the street. I love you."

"Love you too, I'll see you later." We waved goodbye to one another. I picked up my pen to keep grading papers but was quickly interrupted again by a call from King Elementary. I was caught off guard because it was a Saturday and I never got contacted by work on a day off.

"Hello, it's Krystal Jones."

"Hi Krystal, it's Superintendent Jefferson. I apologize to be reaching out to you if you are busy with something, but we need to have a meeting with you."

"It's no problem, sir. What day?"

"Can you meet with us today? Here at the school?"

"Umm yeah, sure, I mean I'm out now, but I'll be free when I drop my mother-in-law off." My voice shook because I was low-key terrified of what they may have wanted. I tried to calm myself down because it probably wasn't something bad. I could be getting an unexpected classroom upgrade, or the principal is getting fired and they want me to step in. Whatever it was, had my full attention so I couldn't wait to get up there.

It took Martha about 30 minutes to get out of the store and I zoomed her to her house to get to the school. I had on a pair of pants and a black casual top so there was no need to change. When I pulled into the parking lot, I saw that there were a few cars up here, one I knew was the principal's. That was starting to make me believe even more that something was going on with her.

When I walked into the school I went into the front office where the conference room was. The door was left open, so I walked into the room and all eyes were on me.

"Mrs. Jones, thank you for coming. You may close the door and have a seat." He directed me, as I shut the door.

"How is everyone doing today?" I asked, attempting to play it cool.

"We're okay." Mr. Jefferson responded as everyone else sat with an uncomfortable look on their face.

"So, to get things started I want to start by saying this is a very uncomfortable situation for everyone here today. We wish to have met under different circumstances but what we saw could not be ignored or put off for another day." He made my stomach start to hurt.

"Mrs. Jones, there was a rumor going around campus that students have been breaking into the textbook room to replace books that they have misplaced throughout the school year. We had campus security go through the cameras for the textbook room and when they did, they found some rather unflattering footage of you doing inappropriate things inside the room during school hours. For this reason, we will be letting you go and suspending you indefinitely from the Dallas Independent School District." When he was done speaking, I was so shocked I had zoned out.

"Mrs. Jones, we have your termination paperwork here and will need for you to sign it." Principal Witiker's annoying ass slid a piece of paper across the desk to me. I couldn't look anyone in the face, so I took the pen and signed my name. There was no need to argue about it because I knew it was true. All those years in college were now gone down the drain because I wanted to be a freak during school hours.

Dammit Nick, you got me humiliated.

Chapter 5

Tish

12:00 pm

My sister and I sat in the living room, both leaning against the armrest of my couch. She hadn't said anything in hours and neither had I. We spent a lot of time here together just in each other's presence. Sometimes she didn't want to go home, and I didn't want her to. She was one of the last few family members I had, and I cherished her even more.

When the front door opened, Chill came in the door with a box of pizza. He's been trying to get me to eat for the past few hours, so his final trick was to get one of my favorite foods.

"Hey mama, you want me to put a few slices on the plate? It's double pepperoni."

"No, I'm okay baby. I'm still not hungry."

"Well, I am." Tasha interrupted me.

"Give me two slices and some ranch please."

"You got it." Chill laughed before going into the kitchen. Not only had he been there for me, but he was opening up a lot with my sister. He told me she was the funniest person he ever met. Nick liked her too; I saw them playfully flirting around sometimes. Too bad they couldn't act on it because he was fucking Krystal. That's however something that a lot of people didn't know, and I wasn't one to tell my friends business. Especially with what she has going on with Leon.

After Chill fixed Tasha's plate, he gave it to her and went back towards the room. Just like Noelle I couldn't help but follow him into the next room. Anywhere he was in the house, I wanted to be. If I could live in Chill's skin, I would. Not to be dramatic but I'm not sure how I ever lived without him. It's as if I breathe better around him and my mind was more at peace.

When I walked into the room, I noticed Chill had the light on in the restroom. Cracking the door, I peeked my head inside and spotted Chill standing in the mirror and flossing his teeth.

He turned around and signaled for me to come into his arms once he saw me there. His embrace was so powerful and comforting that I felt like a kid with him. I used to get this same feeling when I would hug my daddy back in the day.

"So, your birthday is coming up. You want to do anything special?"

"Yeah, do you, that's about it." That made him chuckle.

"That sounds fun but that ain't enough. We can do anything you want. Go anywhere around the world. Your friends can come too. Just say it and it's done."

"Friends?" I raised an eyebrow and then shrugged my shoulders.

"You know I only have one friend at this point and that's Krystal." I put my face against his chest.

"Mama, you got two friends. Don't just push Dixon out like that. Don't get me wrong, I understand your anger towards her but maybe one day you could let it go. I've seen you two together. Y'all real friends. That situation was foul but learn to forgive and forget. Me keeping built-up anger inside hurt me at the end of a lot of shit. Not trying to tell you what to do, just speaking from experience."

He held the small of my back as I looked into his eyes. This beast had some beauty in him, and it was so mesmerizing to see. I couldn't help but take what he said to heart.

"I know everything you're saying is right Chill, it's just hard to accept it. I still blame her partially for what happened with my dad. I mean I know it was his decision at the end of the day but." I paused because I knew I was about to contradict myself.

"I guess I'll have to learn to get over it. Learn to move past it. Forgive and forget right?"

"That's my girl." He squeezed me in his muscular frame.

"But hold on Dr. Phil. When are you going to forgive Keys for whatever happened between you two?"

"Who said this was about me? We talking about you." He flashed a smile.

"Me and Keys good though, I just need my distance for a minute."

"Well, if I eventually speak to his wife then you will be speaking to him too."

"Alright, I can do that." he grabbed a hand full of my ass. While we had time to talk without Noelle in the room, I decided to bring up something else that had been bothering me for some time now.

"Chill, what if I want to work?"

"Work?"

"Yeah, I mean I'm just sitting here every day. I have nothing to take my mind off of the bad things happening and I feel like some type of responsibility would help."

"Work where Tish?" He tore his face up. Chill didn't want me or Noelle picking up a crumb off the floor, let alone working. I mean I loved that he held us on a pedestal, but I was still a human. I'm not a bougie bitch and I can't change that for no amount of money.

"I don't know where, but I can find a job. Maybe do something part-time at the mall or something."

"The mall?" He sounded even more disgusted.

"Why can't I just buy you a Mall and you run that mutha fucka?"

"Chill, no." I laughed at him and his offer.

"Baby that is not the same. I told you that type of stuff is not needed because it's not what impresses me. I just want a hobby at the least. Get out of this penthouse sometime."

"What about a painting class or something."

"I would like that. Sounds relaxing enough for me."

"Okay, you got it. I'll set you up somewhere to go tomorrow."

"Yay, I freaking love you." I reached up to kiss his lips saying the L word for the first time. I didn't mean to say it. It just slipped out. I held my hand over my mouth before Chill removed it and placed his lips on mine.

"Don't be embarrassed baby. I love you too." He responded, sending chills up my spine. Chill hadn't ever told me he loved me, but I knew he did a long time ago. No one takes care of another person like this without love.

I heard the room door open and little feet against the marble floor.

"Hey, Daddy baby." Chill's face lit up as soon as Noelle came into the restroom.

"Hi Daddy, hi Mommy."

"Hi, pretty girl." I kissed her little chunky cheeks.

"Did you have a good nap?"

"Yes, I had a dream about Disney World."

"Is that a hint that you want to go?" Chill asked his spoiled-ass daughter. I was admiring my family when my sister burst into the room with a scared look on her face.

"Chill! Tish! Get out here! The police are trying to break down the door!" She yelled making us hurry into the front. By this time the living room was swarmed with police officers in bulletproof vests, and guns pointed out.

"Malachi, get on the ground now!" They yelled at Chill as they surrounded him.

"For what!"

"What the hell is going on?" I screamed terrified by Chill.

The cops rushed Chill and threw him onto the floor as they pushed us to the side.

"Man, y'all mutha fuckas didn't have to come do this shit in front of my family! What the fuck is this about?" Chill questioned the cops who didn't attempt to answer his question.

"What is he being arrested for!"

"Y'all bogus as hell for coming in here like this!" Tasha added.

"Listen, we need y'all to stand back!"

"Tell me what he's being arrested for! Why can't y'all tell me?"

"Look, you will find out soon enough." They stood Chill on his feet. Once they escorted him out of the penthouse I fell to my knees. What the fuck just happened?

Jesus, I can't take anything else.

Chapter 6

Chill

Two hours later

Jail wasn't for a boss nigga like me, so I knew I had to get out of here ASAP for my sanity. The only problem is, I had no idea why I was here.

The police left me in the room for a few hours until they came bursting in trying to intimidate me. With a clipboard and smug look on their faces, they sat down across from me as if this was a business meeting.

"Mr. Saint, or Chill, which one would you like to be addressed by?"

"Addressed by y'all? Nothing. I don't like to be addressed by niggas I don't fuck with."

"Well, sir." He took a brief pause as he sat the clipboard down on the table which had a brown envelope attached to it.

"Unfortunately, because of these photos, you have no choice but to be addressed by us."

He opened up the envelope and started laying the pictures out one by one. Looking at them I quickly realized what they had but I kept my poker face on. I couldn't let them see me sweat.

"Do you know who these people are in this picture?"

"Nope. Why would I know three dead white boys?"

"Well, to make matters quite frank, you know them because you killed them in Vegas this past December. This one right here was supposed to get married the weekend he went missing." He pointed to one of the dead men.

"Damn, I see he got cold feet." I sat back in my seat with a smirk on my face.

"Don't get smart with me. You know why he didn't get married. You put a bullet in his head after he visited your nightclub."

"And how you figure that?" I leaned in towards him because he wasn't intimidating shit.

"I know because their bodies were found when a fire broke out at the crematorium you own. When the firefighters put out the fire, they found them inside a freezer stacked up like old tuna. Once we pulled records on who they were we found out that they were at your nightclub and no report of them going back to their hotel room after. Of course, your surveillance system at the club was wiped clean, but the men purchased a five-thousand-dollar section there. Now we've done some research on you and a lot of people close to you go missing."

"And?"

"And we believe that you've been killing these people and burning their bodies inside this crematorium. Only these three guys didn't get burned for some reason and were left stacked up in a freezer. Now this wouldn't have been concerning if this crematorium hadn't been registered as closed the past ten years.

"That's it, that's all y'all got? Speculation. Look sir I'm worth 1.2 billion dollars. I own a lot of places all over the world so I'm sure this isn't the first time you've found a body at one of them. I have no idea why their bodies were found there. I haven't been to that place since I purchased it. I've never even stepped foot on that property." I lied with a straight face.

The crematorium was where I sent bodies to be cremated any time, I needed them gone but I didn't do the dirty work. To my knowledge them white boys we're supposed to have been dealt with a long time ago. To leave them piled up like that was some fuck ass shit and I have a feeling the same mutha fucka who let that fall through is the same person Shadow was about to out before Keys killed him.

"I'm not sure about that Chill. We have reason to believe you've been operating that business for the black market. Making bodies disappear."

"Nah, I wouldn't do that."

"Stop the lies!"

"Nigga, I don't lie to anybody. Lying is a form of weakness to me."

"We have reason to believe otherwise. We are learning a lot about you, Chill."

"Did y'all learn that I have a big dick that could have both of y'all's bitches screaming my name? Did you learn that?"

"That's irrelevant sir."

"And so is this conversation. Look, am I being arrested right now?"

"No, not yet." You could see his face turning red having to admit that.

"Well, if that's the case then unlock that door so I can leave. Y'all don't have shit on me so why did y'all waste my time? Let me guess, y'all wanted, a confession?" I laughed in their face.

"You may as well. We will eventually get you, Chill."

"Eventually may never come. Now let me out this mutha fucka." I stood up from the table. Defeat was all over their face and one of them stood up to escort me out. I wasn't sure what I would be doing to get this off my back just yet, but I would come up with something. I damn sure can't go down for killing three white men. I would get the needle for sure for that shit.

When I got to the lobby of the police station, I had to use their phone to call a ride. The lady sitting behind the counter was typing fast on her computer until she looked up at me.

"Can I help you?" She asked while taking her hand through the bottom of her weave. I've noticed any time I talked to women they fidgeted with themselves. Fix their hair, checked a mirror, sucked in their guts. I could make the most comfortable women, insecure.

"I need to use a phone Ms."

"Ms.? It's Sergeant Allen."

"You Sergeant Allen, but you behind a desk, why?"

"Because I got shot six times. Any more questions."

"Nah, none other than can I use your phone." She smirked, sliding her chair over to the phone.

"Here. Keep it short. We don't need the lines tied up."

"Oh, it will be. People move quickly for me." I replied.

I dialed Nick's number because I didn't want to bother Tish with coming out. He was still in Dallas, and I wasn't surprised by that. He was going to go wherever I went and to be honest, I liked it that way. I needed to look out for him.

"Hello."

"Yo, this Chill. The police done talking to me, come scoop me."

"Alright, but whose number is this?"

"The police."

"Alright, say no more." He hung up the phone because he knew our conversation couldn't go any further. I gave the phone back to the cop and then started to walk away.

"You're welcome," she said, and I shrugged my shoulders. I don't thank anybody associated with the people who drugged me out of my house for nothing.

I walked out of the front door hearing her scoff loudly and call me an ass hole. She wasn't the first mutha fucka to refer to me as that and definitely wasn't going to be the last.

I waited on the corner for my brother for about thirty minutes until he sped up like he wasn't in front of the police station. When I got in the car it was smoked out and this nigga had a sack of weed in his cup holder.

"I'm sure I'll be picking you up from here next. Nigga you do remember that you're in Texas right."

"How can I forget? I see a Muh fuckin cowboy hat everywhere I go. Why the fuck did they pick you up bruh?"

"They trying to put a few bodies on me."

"The ones we caught?" His eyes enlarged.

"Nah, other ones. But they don't know shit. They just fuckin with a nigga because they can. Matter of fact, let me see your phone. I got some consequences to dish out back in Vegas."

"Who are you calling? Didn't all your go-to men go back to Chicago when you left?"

"Not all of them. Keys may still be there. Siri call Keys." I spoke into Nick's cell phone. Keys had been on the bench long enough, so it was time to put that nigga back in the game.

When the call was connected, Keys answered the phone breathing hard as hell. I knew this nigga must've been fucking.

"Hello?"

"Yo, this Chill. You in Vegas?"

"Yeah, just got back yesterday."

"Well, I need you to check on some shit for me."

"Alright, tell me what you need." He jumped back in line like it was nothing. The thing about us men, is we don't have to do much talking to get over shit. Females on the other hand need years and counseling.

"You know our hitters that work at the club?"

"Yeah."

"Well, then niggas left some bodies on the cremation table and got me caught up."

"Say no more. I'm going to figure out who, what, and why. But can I call you back when I get in the car? I'm in some pussy right now." He made me chuckle.

"Alright. You and your wife do your thing."

"Pshhh. This is not wifey but I'm for show doing my thing. Stay safe my boy. I'll get back to you in no time."

"Alright. Peace." We hung up the phone.

"That nigga ain't ever gone change." Nick shook his head laughing at Keys.

"One day he will trust me. Y'all just have to run into the right girl."

"To be honest, I think I have. The only problem is I ran into two right girls."

"Krystal and who?"

"You don't know her." He did a menacing smirk.

"Mm, well I hope you make the right decision. The wrong bitch can fuck up your life."

"Don't I know it." He replied but I wasn't sure if he was actually agreeing. Just like me, he would have to learn about these bitches one day. Hoes like that crazy bitch Monique made me appreciate Tish even more.

When I got back to the house, I saw the door had been fixed and walked inside.

"Daddy!" Noelle ran to me and jumped into my arms. I held her tightly and walked into the living room where Tish was sitting on the couch.

"Chill, what was that about? What happened?" She asked, and I held the side of her face.

"It was a mistake mama, it was nothing. We good, and I'm good." I downplayed the situation.

"You promise? I was so worried, and I didn't know what to do. I mean I was already sad and worried about our babies, and I just wanted to know you were good." She rambled off and I caught the word babies.

"Wait, you just said our babies? What babies? We only have one, right?" I crouched down to her height to look her in her eyes. She took a deep breath and then walked away from me, almost doing a jog to the bathroom. When she came back into the room, she had a white plastic stick in her hand that she gave to me with a lopsided smile.

"I wanted to tell you in a cuter way this time. But I just accidentally ran my big mouth. After you got arrested, I started throwing up and Tasha suggested I may be pregnant. She had a test in her purse, so I took it about an hour ago and it turns out I am pregnant Chill." She forced a lopsided smile.

"You for real? My baby boy on the way?" she started to laugh.

"I don't know if it's a boy but it's definitely coming." She smiled and rubbed her stomach. To get news like this after a day like today was needed. Now I had to make sure I was free to raise my son because I for shit sho can't do it properly behind bars.

Chapter 7

Nick

6:00 pm

After I dropped Chill off at home, I went to chill with Tasha. The parking over here was foul so the closest I could park to her was three buildings over.

When I climbed up her stairs, I heard music blasting from inside her apartment. I knocked on the door calmly at first until I started to bang because she hadn't heard me.

When the door finally opened, she stood there smiling at me with her eyes half closed.

"Oh, hey baby come in. These hookers were just leaving." I walked inside the house where two other bitches were sitting on the couch. One of them looked like a gerbil but the other one was alright, I guess.

I hugged Tasha around her waist and then squeezed on her booty as I always did.

"I missed you. Is your brother good? My sister was so upset today. I didn't want to leave her."

"Yeah, he's out. You know that nigga never down for long."

"Good. You can go wait in my room. I'll be in there in a second."

"Alright and hurry up."

I walked towards her room only stopping in my tracks when I saw some crushed-up powder on the dining room table. I spent enough time in Vegas nightclubs to know exactly what this was.

"Tasha."

"Yes."

"What's this about?" I pointed at the lines next to the debit card.

"Oh, this is nothing. It's just some medicine for my headache."

"And you have to crush it up? What kind of medicine is it?"

"Tylenol." Her eyes switched back and forth.

"Who do you think you lying to Tasha? Do I look like a priest or some shit?" I squinted my eyes because she was losing her mind. I may smoke weed but that was as far as I would go. Anything else was crackhead shit to me. Call me a hypocrite but I don't give a fuck. This bitch was over here on crack as far as I'm concerned.

"Okay, Nick. It's cocaine. The girls brought this over to calm me down. You know I've been having a hard time relaxing and getting out of my head." She finally admitted the truth.

"So, this is what kind of friends you have. Trying to help you cope with grief by drugging you up?"

"They are not drugging me up, Nick. Stop being dramatic." She grabbed at my dick, and I backed away.

"No, you stop being dumb. This type of shit is not cool Tasha. I know you hurting but coke is only a temporary high. You'll be selling everything you got to make yourself feel better sooner or later."

"Nick, I said it's not that serious. I'm not going to get hooked on this shit."

"That's what every crackhead on the streets said. I can't believe you. Your ass is nothing like your sister. She would never do any shit like this. She strong, yo ass weak."

I gave it to her straight up because she needed to hear it.

She didn't have anything to say at that point, so I went to curse her ugly ass friends out.

"Y'all bitches need to get the fuck up out of here right now!"

"Excuse me. Who are you talking to?" Alvin's chipmunk got buck.

"Bitch you heard what I said. Y'all hoes ain't no friends of Tasha and y'all need to go. Why would y'all bring drugs over here instead of words of comfort? She lost her father, not a crack pipe."

"She's not doing no fucking crack. It's just a little bump to take the edge off."

"If you don't get the fuck out, I will take the rest of your edges off! The little you got left!"

"Fuck you, crazy ass nigga!"

"Yeah, get to stepping." I opened the door and they both stormed out of the apartment.

"Nick, was that really necessary? I don't even feel high anymore."

"I know you don't. You get high fast and come down even faster on coke. Listen I'm not about to watch you go down a hole so many people back home in Chicago do. You can't turn to hard drugs because of losing someone."

"I wasn't, I just did it this one time."

"One time is how it starts shawty. Think about the first time you smoked weed. Fast forward to now, you probably didn't think you would smoke it every day."

"Well, I wanted to not feel for the moment. I wanted it to all go away, Nick. I mean it does sometimes. Most of the time I'm with you the pain doesn't hurt as bad. But when you're not around I hurt. I hurt so bad sometimes I cry until I throw up." She replied as tears welled up in her eyes. She never really cried around me, so I wasn't used to seeing this side of her. It was like she was hiding her emotions from me which I didn't understand why.

"I can't say I know how you feel but I know that putting shit up your nose ain't the way. Crying is not bad while you grieving. It's the release your body needs."

"If my body needs it then why do I feel so exhausted from it? Why is it I can't sleep sometimes because I'm up crying?"

"Better you can't sleep because you are crying than sleeping forever because you're dead. Baby girl these drugs out here be laced with so much shit. A trace too much of fentanyl and you dead leaving your sister by herself. It's as simple as that."

"You say that as if I'm a junky."

"You aren't, yet. But you'll be riding bikes in old wigs in the next year if you keep it up." She tried not to, but she couldn't help but laugh. Her ass was goofy just like me.

Besides the sex, I was growing to like Tasha. Being around her was almost like hanging with a female version of myself. Though we had this bond I felt as if I still had one with Krystal too. She was the opposite of Tasha in every way, but it still worked for me. In a perfect world, I would continue dealing with them both but for some reason, I knew it would never happen. Trying to split my days between the two of them was becoming too hectic already.

"Can we just go get something to eat now? I'm hungry." She griped as she crossed her arms.

"Yeah, I guess, what you want to eat crackhead? I didn't know y'all got the munchies too."

"Nick stop!" She pouted her lips.

"I'm just fucking with you, what you want?"

"Rudy's."

"Alright, put your shoes on and come on." I reached on the counter for my keys to leave out of the door. I walked down the steps and through a pack of crusty-ass niggas posted up at the bottom. They all made sure to make eye contact with me when I came through and I knew that was an intimidation tactic. That's why I didn't drop my head or look away. Not one of them niggas scared me.

"Hey, Tasha." One of them spoke.

"Hey."

"When can I come upstairs with you?"

"Nah baby girl, fuck that nigga. When can I come?"

All of them started being thirsty as fuck and honestly pissing me off. I walked back to their group and stood amongst all of them.

"So y'all niggas on some disrespectful shit I see?"

"Nick, come on, let's go." Tasha started pulling me away from them.

"Nah, I'm trying to figure out why they talking to you while I'm in reaching distance."

"Reaching distance? Nigga who the fuck is you."

"Don't worry about who I am. Just know that this is mine and y'all don't have shit to say to her." I lifted my shirt to show them my gun.

"Okay lil nigga, we didn't know. But you better calm your bitch ass down." One of the niggas ran his mouth. Without thinking twice, I swung at the nigga knocking him against the car before grabbing my pistol out of my waistband. The rest of his homies backed away with their hands in the air.

"Now like I said, she belongs to me and there ain't going to be no more disrespect. I'm not the nigga to play with. Now get the fuck from in front of her steps." They all scattered like mice as I continued to my car.

"Nick, I can't believe you!"

"Tasha, I don't want to hear you saying I was wrong. Them niggas disrespectful." I replied getting in my car.

"And you were not wrong. I'm not saying anything bad about it. That thug ass shit you did back there was sexy as fuck!"

"Well, what is it that you can't believe?"

"You saying that I belong to you. Do I Nick?"

"I mean, what do you think? Am I not with you every day? Do I not do shit with you and for you?" I replied, and she climbed across the seat to kiss me. I didn't want to make things official just yet, but my emotions put me in the position to have to.

"I'm happy to hear that boo. I promise to keep it real with you."

"And likewise. Now put your seatbelt on Coke'y the bear."

She smacked her lips before laughing and sitting back in the passenger seat so I could take off.

I took her to this little chicken spot she asked for and ordered her chicken. Once we got back to her apartment, we sat on her couch, and she curled up under me while eating it. We didn't have the television on, so the room was fairly quiet. I was just enjoying being next to her warm soft body.

Once she was done, she got up to throw away her trash and then came back to place her head on my chest. She started to rub her hands across my abdomen, then she cleared her throat to speak.

"Nick?"

"What's up?"

"Thanks again for saying everything you said earlier. I know I gave you push back but you were telling the truth. I didn't need to be doing that."

"You didn't but I understand why. You fail to peer pressure which we all have before." I grabbed her chin to look me in the eyes.

"In the future, if you want to feel better just call me. I know what to do to take your mind on a trip to Mars. And it's not just sexual either. We can do things, go places, enjoy each other."

"You mean like go on dates since we're together now."

"Exactly."

"You for real? We're together together?" Her eyes lit up like a child at Disney World.

"Yes, what did I just say? We are together together."

I lifted her chin and kissed her on her lips. I went in for just a peck, but she started tonguing me down within seconds. We kissed for a good lil' minute until she stopped to remove her top. After that, her pretty pink nipples were looking at me eye to eye and I took them into my mouth like pieces of candy. She reached down into my sweatpants and grabbed my dick out the top. She then licked her hand and then started jerking my dick so gently. I tugged at her leggings, and she finally stood up and pulled them down.

I grabbed her small waist and made her turn around so I could kiss all over her big juicy ass. I kissed on the outside, then put my tongue in between her cheeks.

"Fuck, baby." She let leave her lips as I traced my tongue around her peach. Spreading her ass cheeks apart I started to kiss her pussy and her sweet juices dripped down my chin. I was eating her pussy up until the front door suddenly opened, and in came three masked men.

Tasha started to scream before one of them put their gun up to her head.

"Bitch shut the fuck up before I blow your brains out. Nigga give me all the jewelry, clothes, and money you got on you!"

He yelled at me.

My gun was all the way on the counter, so it couldn't do anything to save me right now. It sucks that I'm probably about to die right with my dick out and I didn't even get a nut.

Tragic

Chapter 8

Dixon

The next morning

Getting myself and three kids ready this morning was the most hectic thing I've ever done. Keys woke up with the lord on his mind and said he wanted to go to his favorite church down here. To be honest I wanted to stay at the hotel until they got back but what kind of wife and step-mama would I be? My peace and relaxation time was no more with these newfound duties I had. Now I was ready to break into that jail and help Stella get out to get her children.

Once I was done getting them dressed, I sat them on the couch and went to the patio where Keys was sitting. I walked up to the side of him, and he reached up to rub my ass.

"We're all ready."

"Cool." He stood up from the chair and pulled me close to him.

"Yo Dix, I just wanted to say thank you for stepping up with the kids. Getting them dressed today, going shopping for them, and keeping them while I handled business yesterday. I appreciate you."

"You know I got you, baby. Your kids are my kids now."

I smiled as I grabbed his chin.

"Yeah, well come on let's roll. We want to get a good parking spot. This church be packed."

"Okay, right behind you babe."

Keys and I grabbed the kids and went to the car parked downstairs. We didn't have any car seats here, so we had to ride illegally for the moment. The car ride was rather hectic with the boys fighting and his daughter whining as she'd been doing the entire time.

"Say, y'all lil niggas better stop fighting." Keys kept yelling to the backseat.

"Princess, do you want to come sit up here with me?" I looked back to Keys daughter who was stuck in the middle of a war.

"No! I don't like you." She said, and I almost told her I didn't like her either, but I had to remember she was a child. I'm happy we are on our way to church because I needed some prayer in my life.

Back in Dallas, I attended a megachurch that was just as big as an NBA arena. So of course, I had my nose turned up when Keys pulled into this small shack on the outskirts of Vegas. There were cars surrounding it, so I guess it was a good place to be. Plus, all the large hats and women in church suits meant there was some good church had up in here.

When we walked inside, everyone turned over their shoulders, some smiling and some turning their nose up at us. Keys walked us to the second row where there was an opening big enough for our family.

"How you doing brother?" An older gentleman behind our row stood up to greet Keys.

"I'm good, thanks for asking bruh. How have you been?"

"I'm good I'm good. Glad to see these little ones again." He pinched one of the boys on his cheek.

"And this is?" The gentleman put his attention on me.

"Oh, this is my wife Dixon. Dixon this is Avery Cartwright. He's a deacon here at the church."

"Hi, nice to meet you." I was still smiling because of Keys calling me his wife. The choir's organist started to play a tune and everyone's attention went to the pulpit. We all stood and clapped along to the music while the choir sang their opening selection.

I know Jesus, He will fix it for you

For He knows just what to do, oh

Whenever you pray, let Him have His way.

After they finished two songs, an older lady did church announcements and then it was time for the pastor to preach. He started off the sermon by telling us to look to our neighbors and say we are worth it.

"We are worth it." Keys and I said to one another. We then gave our full attention to the pastor as he went into the scripture and then began preaching the word. The church was small but there was a strong holy presence in the pulpit. The higher his voice rang, the more he seemed to reach the audience. I for one was so moved that I stood up along with other church members raising their hands and shouting. By the time he was calling people to the altar for special prayer, I was all in. Especially after looking at Keys and seeing tears in his eyes. Me and my baby were feeling this message today.

I grabbed his hand and we both walked up to the pulpit joined by a few others. We were instructed to bend to our knees and the pastor would come by and say a special prayer for us. The entire time he was making his rounds Keys and I held hands, so I felt like we were as one right now. My eyes were closed tightly, and I was ready for a blessing. That was until a powerful punch hit the back of my head sending pain down my spine. I stood up in a daze, turning around to see Stella throwing another punch straight to my face knocking me down. When the fuck did this bitch get out?

"Yeah, you thought you were safe because you got me locked up huh? Well, I'm out bitch. Get your ass up." She said and the crowd roared with "Ouuuu's and Unt Unts."

She tried swinging at me once again, but I blocked it with my forearm.

"Really Stella, you're going to do this in here?"

"Xavier, you had no business bringing her here. You know I showed you this place!"

"You don't own this church. Stella, you tripping bruh!"

"I'm tripping? No, you tripping! I spent months in behind bars because of this bitch! Now you got her up in my church with my kids!"

"Girl fuck you and your kids!"

The crowd roared again but I didn't give a damn. She had me heated putting her hands on me yet again. I turned to Keys,

"I'm about to get up out of here! You need to control your baby mama, or we're done!" I attempted to walk away before she grabbed me by my ponytail. She pulled me down to the ground and started swinging on me even more until I grabbed her leg and made her fall to the ground with me. I climbed on top of her and started punching her in her face with my fist as hard as I could. Keys and other members started pulling me off of her and I didn't stop swinging until we were completely separated.

"I'm calling the police so your ass can go back to jail!" I yelled towards her who was holding her bloody nose.

Once the deacon who grabbed me off of her put me down, I jetted out of the church hoping to get away from that crazy bitch.

"Stella, you need to chill!" I turned and saw Keys attempting to hold Stella back. She hadn't had enough.

"No! I'm not chilling! This hoe caused me to miss months with my kids! Had them living like God knows what and you didn't even try to get them until it was too late!"

"Don't blame me! Nobody told you to jump on that girl!"

"You told me when you decided to marry the bitch behind my back!"

"I told you it was a mistake!" He made me stop in my tracks to address him.

"A mistake? I'm glad to know you still feel that way Keys!" I yelled because my feelings were hurt.

"Of course he does bitch! You not the type that can lock a nigga down!"

"Yeah, but I locked you down! How did that small ass cell feel?" I smirked to piss her off and did just that.

She charged at me again and we were going blow for blow until Keys finally got us separated.

"You mutha fuckas stop! What the fuck is wrong with you bitches? Fuckin stop!" Keys yelled so hard veins were protruding from his forehead.

"Keys shut the fuck up! You know why I'm on this bitch ass! We just talked about this last night! You remember, before you shot nut into my pussy!"

"Last night? What the hell does she mean last night? You been talking to her Keys?"

"He was FUCKING me last night, and we talked a little too. What, you thought he was going to leave me alone because of a petty ass ring? Do you know how many bitches got one of those? This dummy is a serial fiancé bitch."

She made my blood boil so hot that I felt my body start to sweat.

"None of that matters because I'm calling the cops on you bitch."

Keys grabbed for my hand.

"Keys get off of me!"

"Stop, don't call them, please."

"So, you're protecting her now? You know what, fuck you too Keys!" I walked away as he followed.

"Dixon wait."

"No, let her go! Why are you telling her to wait? Me and your kids are ready to go home!"

"You heard her Keys. Go be with your real family because I'm just a mistake right."

He dropped his head.

"You could've told me she was out of jail so I could've watched out for myself."

"I didn't know she was out until I picked the kids up from CPS and she called my phone on the way home. I swear I just found out last night."

"Keys none of that even matters now. Be with your family. I'm done."

"Come on dummy before the cops come! Let's go!" Stella yelled from behind him.

Keys dropped his head and shook it back and forth in a battle which was honestly enough for me. I was his wife; I should be an automatic pick but obviously, I'm not. I've had fights in my lifetime, but I never thought I would have to fight over my husband. And in a church at that. This bitch Stella would go to no end to prove her point. I don't want to do this for the rest of my life. My heart is already broken now.

"You know Keys, you messed up something really good for that headache you call a baby mama. She can have you for real. I'm done being loyal to someone who doesn't love me." I turned to walk away.

This time, he didn't follow me or say anything else and that shattered my already broken heart. I don't know why I believed he was for me when all the signs were saying differently.

Fuck, how could I be so stupid? Why the fuck did I stay married to him?

Chapter 9

Krystal

The next day

I just couldn't handle my kids rights now, so I took them to my Mother's Day care as if I had to work. All day I sat up in the house, crying my eyes out, and physically cringing from embarrassment. Knowing that I was seen like that made my head hurt. I'm sure I would be the talk of the entire school, shit the town if that video got out. That's why every time my phone rang; I thought it was someone saying my story was on the internet. The one thing I was dreading the most was my mom and dad finding out. I would never be able to show my face to them again.

I still didn't know what I would tell them about my job and how I would break it to them that I was unemployed. I wasn't going to be able to afford this house anymore. Especially with Leon's bitch ass in the wind. I can't wait to file child support on his punk ass just like his side bitch did.

As I sat there, I got angrier and angrier. I needed to be talked off the edge but the person I wanted to hear from hadn't answered me yet. I dialed Nick's number for the 50th time today but still, he didn't pick up.

When his phone went to voicemail yet again, I slammed my phone down on the arm of my couch. Maybe he was busy doing something important but then again, I couldn't help but think the worst about his disappearance. He usually texts me good morning and good night faithfully so I hope he was okay.

    Once the sun started to set, I knew I had no choice other than to go get the kids. I didn't put on clothes and walked outside in my pajamas. The daycare was about fifteen minutes away from my house and I listened to Not Gon Cry by Mary J Blige on repeat the whole way there. When I pulled up, I saw my mama waving to one of her kids leaving out of the door and her eyes bucked when she saw my appearance.

"Krys baby are you sick? Why are you dressed like that, and where is your bra? Did you work today?"

"Mama, I went home after work because I had a headache. I'm just out to get the kids and I'm going back home, dang."

"Hold on now, wait just a minute. Who are you talking to like that?"

My mama placed her hand on her hip. I was grown but I still knew the look she was giving me meant to straighten up.

"I'm sorry mama. I'm just sleepy and this headache is killing me." I touched my temple.

"Krystal, I told you not to let Leon missing drive you crazy. He will come back one day just as he did the last time. Look, go sit in my office and relax for the next ten minutes while I get the kids ready to go. There are some peppermints under the counter." She moved to the side to let me in the door.

Ever since I was a child, my mama gave me peppermints to calm me down or cure any illness I had. She tricked my mind into believing that the coolness in my mouth could calm down my entire body and make everything else feel better. I know it sounds silly now, but deep down I feel like it worked. A peppermint a day will keep the pain away as my mama always said.

I reclined back in her chair as I sucked on a mint with my eyes closed. I was chilling in my own vibe until her office phone started to ring on the desk. I wasn't going to answer it at first until I thought about my mama getting on to me.

"Second Home Day Care facility," I picked up the phone.

"Hello, is this Mrs Harper?"

"No, this is her daughter. I can help you with what you need."

"Oh, okay. I was just calling to let her know I'm going to be in traffic for a minute. I will probably be about thirty minutes late to pick up my daughter, but I'll tip her again for staying late."

"Okay, I will let her know. What's the child's name?"

"It's Leona, Leona Vincent."

"Okay, got it. I'll go tell her now."

"Okay, thanks, Krystal." She replied, before hanging up the phone. I scrunched my nose up because I didn't expect her to say my name. I guess my mama has been running her mouth about me to her.

I rolled the chair back from the desk and walked to the toddler classroom to talk to my mom.

"Hey mama, Leona's mama called and said she was going to be late today. She's in traffic." My mama rolled her eyes.

"Not again, that girl is late almost every other day. I mean I don't mind if I don't have anything to do after work but that is not the case today." She seemed frustrated.

"Well, she says she tips you for staying right?"

"Yeah, but your dad is going to be so disappointed our plans are pushed back. He wanted us to go to the movies and see that Color Purple Musical tonight since he will not be off for his birthday."

"Well, just go mama, I'll stay behind and make sure everything is straight."

"Thank you, baby. Let me get everything closed down and then I'll go." She smiled, going out of the room. I went back to her office desk dozing off again until my mama got my attention from the door.

"Okay, shugga, I'm about to go. Call me if you need anything."

"Okay, be careful mommy. Tell Daddy I'll call him early in the morning." I walked her out to the door. When I walked back into the playroom Faith was standing there with her head tilted to the side in curiosity.

"Mama, why do you look like you going to sleep?" She asked, as soon as I picked her up.

"I didn't feel like putting on clothes today. I spent all my energy getting y'all dressed this morning." I started to playfully pinch her little bottom. She squirmed and giggled until I put her down. When I walked up behind LJ, I gave him a big kiss on his forehead. I love both of my kids I swear I do, but my heart skipped a beat looking at my son. LJ was my first unconditional love, and I wanted the moon and the stars for him. He was so handsome, and the perfect mixture of me and his trifling-ass dad.

"And how are you little one?" I gave my attention to the little girl Leona playing with blocks on the ground.

"Her can't talk mommy. Her need you to teach her." Faith chimed in.

"Hi Leona, can you talk baby?"

She shook her head yes.

"Okay, so what do you like to watch? We can put the television on something until your mommy comes."

She looked at the T.V. and then back at me before shrugging her shoulders.

"Put it on Mighty Pups mama," Lj suggested.

"Put it on your favorite movie Baby Boy Mama."

"No faith, go sit down and hush up." She giggled like something was funny. When she got to the slide, she ran up and fell down causing a scene. LJ and Leona both started to laugh, and I had to double-take because for some reason they sounded just alike.

My eyes squinted in curiosity, and I took a second glance at her letting myself start to think off the wall. Why did she kind of have the same eyes as my kids and her little lips were chapped just as Faith's is with no chapstick. She had the same sponge-textured hair as my children and her eyelashes were super long like theirs. Was I tweaking or was this little girl my kid's relative?

"Leona, come here baby."

She walked up to me.

"Hey honey, what's your mommy and daddy's name?" She started to twist in her plats.

"My mommy's name is Ashanti, and my daddy's name is Daddy." She replied, and I saw this wasn't going anywhere.

"Y'all wait right here. I'll be back." I left them right there and went to my mother's file cabinet. I searched through it for Leona's folder and when I found it, I got straight to work. I saw that her address was in North Dallas and her mama's last name was Vincent. I went to Facebook to see if I could find her there. Several Ashanti Vincent's popped up but Leona's face in her profile picture helped me locate the right profile.

I scrolled down her page, and she posted all day every day just like a young bitch. Apparently, her birthday was last month, and she just turned twenty-five. I was scrolling and keeping up until I saw a picture that made me stop in my tracks. It was a photo of her that had a caption saying that she was at work. Her job was a Bombshells in Austin which just happened to be Leon's favorite sports bar down there. When he was driving to San Antonio all the time, he used to brag about stopping there. Every time he carried a load he just had to stop and see his people at Bombshells.

I scooted my chair away from the desk and tried to calm myself down, but I was livid knowing this bitch was trying to play us. Why bring your baby to my mama's establishment out of all the daycares in Dallas? And trust I know it wasn't a coincidence. Leon had to tell her about this place or maybe she had looked me up in the past being nosey. What made me even more mad was that I now knew the bitch who got all my Vegas money. That's why her trifling ass got a new car a couple of months ago.

Oh, hell nah, they all got me fucked up.

Still pissed off, I grabbed her folder again to get her address. Now that I think about it, this could be where Leon's bitch ass was hiding. I was going to catch his ass in the act. I'm going over there now.

I gathered the kids and took them out to my car then burned off from the daycare without even strapping them in. Ashanti's address was twenty minutes out, so I quickly got to her apartment complex going sixty the whole way there.

"Mommy where are we at?"

"Don't worry about it LJ. Just come on." I helped them out of the backseat. The paperwork had apartment forty-two on it, so I followed the slidewalk until I found Ashanti's apartment. There was loud music coming from inside which really made me believe Leon was in there. He was known for blasting music even early in the mornings.

    I beat on the door with my hand and then my fist before turning around to kick at the door. The kids came up beside me, also banging on the door with their badasses. When it finally swung open, there was Ashanti, Mrs stuck in "traffic" standing with a blunt.

"Why are you banging on my door like that?" She tore her face up. I took the blunt out of her fingers and threw it down the sidewalk.

"Bitch what is wrong with you?"

"Oh, shut up! I'm sure my money I bought this weed hoe!"

"What are you talking about?" She tried to play dumb.

"You bought it with all that child support money you got from my husband."

"Mommy," Leona shouted from behind me.

"What are you doing with my child? Leona come here!"

"I was at the daycare watching her for my mother while you were supposedly in traffic. You not though, you just up in this bitch smoking weed with my husband! What kind of woman hides a man from his responsibilities?"

"Listen bitch I don't know what the fuck you are talking about right now but I'm about to call the police because why did you have my child? I left her at the daycare." She attempted to close the door and I pushed inside her apartment. I just knew Leon's no-good ass was in here. I scanned the room only to see a tall skinny dude playing the PlayStation with headphones on. He hadn't even heard the commotion at the door.

"Sean help me get this crazy bitch out of my house. She just had our kid!"

"How? I thought she was at daycare."

"She was! But she's the owner's daughter and she saying I'm sleeping with her husband."

"Because you are, or you did! Look, I know what kind of bitch you are just by looking at you. Filthy, irresponsible, and ghetto past any return. You disgust me."

"First of all, you fuckin lunatic, this is my boyfriend Sean's child."

"And how do you know that?"

"Because I just do. I don't have to explain shit to you."

"Girl stop lying! You fucking Leon and that's how you found my mama daycare. He sent you there!"

"Bitch I only knew about your daycare because of an ad on Facebook."

"Yeah, right bitch."

"You know what, why am I even explaining myself to you? Get your crazy ass out of here and know I'm getting that daycare shut down! Sean help me get her up out of here."

She and her man started to push me out of the door.

"Wait! Wait, so you really don't know where Leon is."

"For the last time lady, I don't know you or your husband. Now get the fuck out! I will be filing a police report. Now go!" She replied, slamming the door.

I grabbed my kids and hurried to the car still breathing heavily. I cranked up my car and pulled away quickly while hitting the steering wheel. Was she telling the truth, and did I just jeopardize my mother's business for nothing? My life was seemingly spiraling day by day and I truly wanted to know what I did to deserve this. I miss the days when I lived a perfect life and when I thought my family was perfect.

This dysfunctional shit was truly driving me insane.

Chapter 10

Tish

When Krystal said she needed to talk I decided to invite her over to my place. Chill hired a caterer to cook us a full spread to celebrate the baby. I'm sure it was going to be too much food to eat.

The entire kitchen was full of appetizers, and entrées set up beautifully on the countertops. There were flowers everywhere, a small fog machine giving a cloud-like illusion, and the smell of delicious seafood floating into my nose.

Chill and I were both dressed, but for some reason, I felt basic as hell next to him. It seemed like no matter what I did to myself, I still never looked as good as Chill. He had an elegance about him that I just didn't carry.

When I walked up to him sitting on the bed fastening his watch, he quickly placed his hand on my belly.

"Are you telling people about the baby yet? Or do you want to keep it between us?" He asked as he rubbed his large hands all over my nonexistent bump.

"I want the people closest to us to know but I'm not concerned with the rest of the world. Krystal is coming over tonight so we can tell her, and I called my sister to invite her over, but she hasn't answered yet. I'm surprised since I mentioned a free meal." I shrugged my shoulders.

"Maybe she's sleeping. You know her ass lazy."

"Yeah, maybe earlier, but I know she hasn't been sleep all day. I've been calling her since yesterday." I replied just as the doorbell rang.

"That's Krystal, I'll go let her in." I walked to the front door. When I opened it, I was greeted with smiles from two of my favorite babies in the whole world.

"Hi, Auntie Tish!" They both hugged me around the bottom half of my body. Me and Krystal hugged each other and I stepped to the side for them to come in.

"Best friend, this place is just, wow." She seemed to be lost for words. Looking at her face, I could tell she had been crying. I'm sure this Leon shit was taking a toll on her. I wish he would get his shit together.

"Faith, how about I take you to Noelle's room to play with her? And LJ, I have something special for you in one of the guest rooms."

"What is it!"

"A play station 5. We got it just for you. You can even take it home when you're done." He started jumping up and down. I grabbed both of their hands and took them down the hall so Krystal and I could catch up.

Once the kids were occupied, Krystal and I went into the kitchen to start on the appetizers. My appetite was at a peak right now, so I filled one of the small saucers up with one of everything.

"Who's all eating this food? I know I'm taking a plate home."

"Yes, girl eat up. The only people I'm expecting are you and Tasha."

"Damn, I can't believe she is not here yet with all of this food. My sister be high and hungry."

"I know, me either. I been calling her. But maybe it's good that she's late because we need to talk. First off, are you okay?"

"I'm doing okay, just taking everything day by day."

"That's good. As long as you aren't driving yourself crazy." I bit into a yummy ass buffalo chicken slider.

"Tish, I could only admit this to you, but I did something stupid earlier." She started to shake her head.

"Something stupid like what?"

"Friend, I showed up at this girl's house who I thought Leon had a kid with."

"What!" My eyebrows raised.

"I don't think it's her though after visiting and I may have ruined my mama's business in the process."

"What does the daycare have to do with it?"

"Long story short, the girl whose house I showed up at, kid comes to my mama's daycare. I took the child from the daycare when I went to confront her."

"Oh, Krystal."

"I know, trust I know that was stupid. I don't know why I let my emotions take over me, but I did. Now when she exposes me and calls the police my mama will lose everything she worked hard for. But this all boils down to Leon and everything he's done to me. He even put his hands on me before he left. It's like he's someone I don't know, and it has me questioning everything we had since college." She quickly got emotional and started to cry. I reached over to her shoulder and rubbed it just as Chill walked into the kitchen. When he saw Krystal crying, he started to slowly back away, but it dawned on me that he could help. Chill was good at making problems go away with both his money and power.

"Babe come here." I waved for him to come back.

"What's going on?"

"Krystal was just telling me she made a mistake and could jeopardize her mama's business if word gets out. What do you think we should do?"

"What did she do?"

"Krys, you want to tell him?" I asked her because I wasn't going to tell her business. I'm not a messy person.

"Yeah so, I showed up looking for my husband and acted crazy at one of the daycare's client's houses. Now the girl is saying she's going to end my mother's business because of me, and I feel so bad."

"Who's the girl? Do you have her address? A phone number?"

"Yeah, that's how I popped up on her."

"Well, I'm not trying to overstep my boundaries but if you need me to help, I will. Just say the word."

"Are you going to kill her?" She asked and he started to chuckle.

"Who do you think I am? Do I seem like a murderer to you?" He asked and after me and Krystal caught eyes we laughed. He couldn't be seriously asking that question. Chill has the most intimidating appearance there is, but don't get me wrong, his ass was still fine with it.

"Anyway, I'll handle it. No bloodshed. Just stop crying. Y'all need to be eating all this food before it gets cold." He got a shrimp from my plate.

"Thank you, Chill. I appreciate you for trying to fix it even if you can't convince her to let it go."

"There's no ifs to it. She will. Stop crying."

Krystal got a tissue and wiped her face before digging into the food. After eating just a few bites and tasting this food, I got the urge to call my sister again. I dialed her number, but when her phone went to voicemail, my appetite was gone just like that.

"Are you okay?"

Krystal asked, holding her hand over her mouth as she chewed.

"No, I mean I'm fine, I'm just really wondering where the hell my sister is. It's not like her to let her phone die."

"Don't you have her location?"

"Yeah, it said she was at home earlier but, that's even more reason of why it's weird that her phone is dead now."

"Should I have gone by there and checked on her before coming here?" Krystal asked, and I started to feel anxious.

"I didn't even think about it at first but maybe we should go ride by there to see what's going on. Maybe she's having a mental breakdown and needs me."

"Yeah, that's true."

"Baby, can you watch the kids while I go check on my sister?"

"Of course, do your thing." He answered in between gulps of the wings he was eating. We quickly left out of the house because my anxiety had convinced me to panic. I was definitely on her ass for even putting me through this being irresponsible.

Once we drove to her place, I was able to park right next to her car. We got out of the car and on my way up the steps I said a quick prayer.

When I knocked on the door it squealed and opened up and my heart started to race.

"Tasha?" I stepped further into the apartment. It was quiet but there was a faint sound of moaning coming from her bedroom. It sounded as if someone was hurt so I hurried into the room with Krystal on my tail.

When we stepped inside the room. I gasped loudly seeing my sister bound and gagged naked on her bed. What was even more shocking was that Nick was beside her, bleeding from the top of his head naked too. What the hell was he doing over here?

"Oh, my God, Krystal help me get them untied." I ran to take the tape off her mouth and she instantly started to cry.

"Tish, thank God you came over here. We been like this since yesterday."

"Do you know who did this to you? Krystal help Nick please." I struggled to get the rope off her wrist. Krystal hadn't moved from the door.

"Krystal, snap out of it. Please come help me get them loose." I begged her and she ignored me once again.

"So, Nick, this is what you've been doing!" She started to yell at him, and the realization hit me quickly. Nick was here with my sister.

"My life is spiraling down a fucking dark hole because of you and you over here with her! Someone who is like a sister to me! You're a fucking dog and you're no different than my fuckin husband!"

She turned and left out of the room. Krystal soon slammed the front door behind her, and Tasha looked at Nick who was still tied up.

"You were fucking her too? Tish leave him tied up."

"Tasha no," I replied to her crazy ass. This shit was way too much drama for a pregnant woman, and I can't be dealing with this stuff like this. I had some major decisions to make about my life and where I wanted to be at this point. Dallas was one bad thing after another.

Chapter 11

Chill

The next day

Tish was chilling in her new favorite spot on our patio. The view from up here was calming, to say the least, and you kind of felt alone in the world up here. When I slid the glass door to step outside, she looked over her shoulder and smiled at me, looking back at the view straight ahead.

"I didn't mean to mess up your vibe. Just wanted to come tell you I'm about to leave for a little bit."

"Handling business?" She asked, sipping from her coffee mug.

I sat beside her on the outdoor sofa she had her favorite blanket laid across.

"Yeah, handling business but nothing dangerous though. Do you need anything while I'm out?"

"Mmm, no, not really. Maybe some more cereal for Noelle and more hot chocolate for me."

"So, my son is craving hot chocolate?"

"Yes and no. I always enjoyed hot chocolate. I guess double now since your kid likes it." She smiled.

"My son."

"Yeah, whatever you say, baby daddy. But I also might need one more thing from you but I'm not sure if you could get it today."

"One more thing like what?"

"A new house, in a new city, and a new state."

I lifted my eyebrow, and she knew she caught me off guard.

"I know, that's going against everything I used to say but things change with the times. Dallas just seems so bad now. It's full of bad memories, and bad people, and I'm ready to get away. Start over fresh. Especially after what happened with our siblings. Which is still crazy to think about."

"So, you're willing to leave your sister?"

"No, I mean with her and your brother together, or whatever they are doing, I feel like we could get her to come too. Rent her a small little apartment near us."

"As you know your wish is my command, I just hope you don't get cold feet or want to come back after we get settled somewhere else."

"I won't." She quickly replied as if her mind were made up.

"I mean I don't hate this city, but I hate the memories you know. It's the kind of place I only want to visit in the future. That way I can appreciate the good without focusing on the bad."

"Yeah. I get what you saying, and as I said your wish is my command." I leaned over to kiss her on her lips.

Little taps started at the glass window and we both knew who it was without turning around.

"It looks like somebody up from their nap. Get ready to talk about her dream for the next ten minutes."

"You know your child," Tish replied, and we both laughed. I got up to open the door for Noelle and she hugged me around my leg before I picked her up to carry her to her mama.

"I'm going to leave now. Start looking for houses in Calabasas or some shit."

"Where the Kardashians live?"

"Yeah, and the Saint's too if you find a place."

"What's my budget?"

"You don't have one. Get what you like. Numbers don't exist for you." She smiled and blew a kiss at me. As they waved by to me, I smiled back happy with what my life had become. I could honestly say I was becoming successful with this family man thing. Only I didn't have to try too hard because it honestly came naturally to me.

Once I got in my Cullinan, I texted Krystal that I needed that address now for her little problem. It only took her a couple of seconds before she sent back an address for me to GPS. I drove to ol girl's house and walked up to her front door.

When I knocked a couple of times it only took a few seconds before the female inside swung the door open. She was a short, biracial-looking chick, with curly brown hair. Cute lil chick but she looked young as hell.

"Are you Ashanti?"

"Yes, who are you?" She looked at me from head to toe.

"I'm Chill Saint, may I come in for a second?"

"Nah, I don't know you enough to let you in. How can I help you? Is Sean fucking your baby mama or something?"

"Nah, Sean not doing that." I snapped having to remember what I came here for.

Look to make a long story short I have an offer for you to keep your mouth closed and drop that little lawsuit and smear campaign you have on that daycare."

"And who are you? Their muscle? Wait, you here to take me out ain't you." She attempted to close the door, but I stopped her.

"No need to run away. I come in peace. I just wanted to offer you something for your silence."

"For my silence? I'm not being silent about anything. That girl could've hurt my baby."

"But she didn't. She just thought her nigga was over here is all. I know you have your fears and scary thoughts about your daughter because I too have them with my little girl. So, to help you kind of move past that and let go of your public accusations I'm offering you fifty thousand to just let it go."

"Fifty thousand what?"

"Pigeons," I replied sarcastically.

"It's money. I have it in my car right now, but I have to hear you call the police station as well as the courts to drop your lawsuit. I also want all those social media posts deleted and for you to never speak about that shit again. It was just an honest mistake on Krystal's behalf." I replied, and she shook her head and leaned against the door frame.

"I don't know. Fifty thousand can't make up for my baby being in harm's way."

"Okay, well let's make it a hundred thousand, but you have to say yes within the next five seconds or it's back down to fifty. Five, four, three, two." I counted.

"Okay, okay I'm with it. A hundred grand could do me justice. Definitely could make up for my baby being kidnapped."

"I wouldn't say kidnapped but that's neither here nor there."

"What else do you call it?"

"I call it Krystal figuring your ass out and attempting to stand on business."

Her eyes started shifting from side to side. I liked to think of myself as a human lie detector and even though it wasn't my business, I still wanted to know was Krystal actually on the right path with her missing baby daddy.

"But she didn't figure shit out."

"I feel like she did. I mean come on, this between you and me. That's her husband's kid ain't it?"

"How you figure that?"

"Because of that female instinct a mutha fucka. If she felt it, it's probably true."

She didn't say anything and just dropped her head. She was silent for a moment before she looked up at me.

"Okay, yes, it is her husband's baby, but I couldn't say anything in front of my man. He didn't even know I filed child support on another man so of course when she came over, I was going to deny it."

"Damn, ain't that something." I shook my head as I started to walk away.

"Wait, when will I get my money?"

"I'll bring it to you after I run to the bank. I only have fifty in the car."

"Okay. Just know the deal is not on until the money is in my hands. All one hundred thousand with no excuse".

I chuckled and shrugged my shoulders.

"Shorty I wouldn't make an excuse for a hundred thousand dollars. That's play money to me."

"And who are you?" She bit her lip sizing me up with her eyes.

"I'm your worst nightmare if you don't do what I say, I'll be back." I walked back to my car to leave. Down the street only through a few lights was a chase bank. I had a few million in an account there so I got the cash and took it back to ol girl's house. When I gave her the money through the door she almost passed out. Some people never saw a hundred thousand dollars in a lifetime.

I left her house and hit the freeway going about eighty in the fast lane. I made it to my street and didn't let off the gas until I saw police lights flashing in my rearview mirror. It wasn't a traditional police car. It was an all-black SUV with no police markings except the lights.

"Here we go with these mutha fuckas again."

I pulled over to the side of the road and let my window down as he approached the car.

When he got to the window, he looked down at me and said,

"Where are you going in such a hurry Chill?"

Because he said my nickname, I knew this wasn't a regular traffic stop. Now I wish I would've never stopped the car and made these mutha fuckas come get me.

Chapter 12

Dixon

After I left Keys at that church with his psycho bitch, I went straight to the airport. It took me six hours to catch a standby flight, and I was unfairly sat by a passenger with a newborn baby. The baby cried the entire flight which gave me a headache that I still couldn't get rid of days later.

I'd used everything in my medicine cabinet for pain, yet I still felt it. Not only did my head hurt but my heart was broken from Keys. Usually in times like this, I would run to my girls for comfort, but our relationships were so strained, that I knew that wasn't an option anymore.

After pacing my floors and lighting every relaxing candle in here I was still bothered by my situation with Keys. I wanted us to work so bad and finding out that he was a snake hurt me to my core. I held secrets for this man, and I went against common sense just to make things seem right in my head.

After sitting on my couch and moving to my bed, then moving to the barstools I knew I wouldn't be comfortable anywhere in here while sober. I needed to be taken out of my misery with as many shots as it would take to get my blood alcohol level too high to drive.

I decided to go to the bar and jumped in the shower to bathe and brush my teeth. I went into my closet and found these black thigh-high boots that I purchased after I had surgery. Being a plus-sized woman in the past, things like thigh-high boots were always unavailable for me. I will say time and time again that getting that surgery was the best decision I ever made in my life. There would be plenty more men where Keys came from. As a matter of fact, tonight I'm going to a spot I knew men with money frequented. Bar Bungalow in downtown.

I put on my thigh-high boots, and a black leather skirt, with a long sleeve gold and black top. After spraying on my favorite perfume, I went to my car and started it for the first time in months zooming off to the bar.

When I got there, I valet parked and went inside turning heads as I strolled through. I sat at the bar and scanned through the menu unsure of what I would get. Since Keys couldn't drink, I hadn't drank in months. I wanted something good, strong, and fruity. Something to be nice going in but ugly coming up.

"Long time no see Ms. Dixon."

The bartender Paul approached me at the counter.

"What can I get for you?"

"I guess I'll take a lemon drop. Sugar on the rim please."

"You got it." He winked his eye, and I smiled back.

When a man sat down next to me, I wasn't paying him any mind until he started talking to me.

"Excuse me, are those good?"

"Is what good?"

"Lemon drops, the drink you ordered."

"I mean I like them."

"Then they must be good. You seem like you have good taste." He smiled, as he took off his suit jacket. He was about 6'0, dark-skinned, and he smelled of my favorite Tom Ford cologne. He had a fade, and waves in his hair like an ocean.

"Chance, what can I get for you?" Paul asked, showing he must've been a regular here.

"I'll have an Old Fashion."

"You got it, captain." Paul saluted him before going to make his drink,

"I've never had an Old Fashion before."

"If you stick around long enough, I'll make that your next drink on me."

"Oh trust, I plan on being here for a while." I giggled like a little girl. Even if I did have plans on leaving, I definitely wouldn't be going anywhere anytime soon. This man was fine, Jack pot.

We sat at the bar and made friendly conversation as drinks were served. I'd learned that he was a pilot from Fort Worth who flew for Delta Airlines. He was newly divorced and had one kid with his ex-wife. Chance and his wife had been married for five years, vs my and Keys's very short-lived marriage. His failed relationships had us talking for hours like old friends. It was nice to speak with a man as eloquent and prestige as Chance. This was the type of man I should be chasing instead of dread-head unloyal thugs.

After some time went by, Chance looked at his Apple Watch.

"It's 9:30 already. I feel like I should be making my way home soon. I have a flight tomorrow at 10:00 am and 200 people are depending on me to make it there on time."

"And God knows if you are late, they will throw a fit." I watched as he put on his jacket. I don't know if it was the liquor or his conversation, but Chance had me wanting him bad.

"Well, it was nice to meet you, Dixon. Do you mind if I get your number to call you sometime?" I quickly became flattered.

"Of course, you can but I could give it to you now in the morning before your flight." I rubbed up his chest.

"Before my flight? You're flying out of town tomorrow too?"

"No silly, I was thinking we could have a nightcap. A quick one though since you have to get to sleep for your flight."

Once he caught on to what I was implying he dropped his head before he nervously laughed.

"I see what you mean." He took a brief pause.

"Look Dixon, you're a beautiful girl and I really enjoyed our time here tonight but unfortunately this is where it ends. I don't have nightcaps with women I just met but of course, if the future presents that opportunity, then I may be more objective to it. But in the future."

"I see." I looked away quite embarrassed, to say the least. I'd never been turned down from a one-night stand before in my life.

"Didn't mean to offend you. It's just where I am in my life right now."

"I can understand that. I didn't mean to jump the gun. I've just been drinking." I put my head down.

"It's okay, you're okay. I understand. I used to get like that too but therapy and talking it out helped me with my addiction. Maybe I can send you some recommendations for a counselor." He spoke as if he just knew I had a sexual addiction. I didn't know whether to be offended or take his advice. I decided to play it cool though.

"Okay, take down my number and shoot me the details." He handed me his phone on the contact screen. I put my number in and gave it back to him.

"I can't wait to hear from you again Captain Chance Suthers." I playfully saluted him. He stuck his hand out to shake mine and then went out of the door leaving his scent behind. Damn, this man is fine.

I didn't leave the bar after him and sat there drinking lemon drop after lemon drop until I was drunk as hell. When it was time for me to go, Paul was concerned about me driving so he called me an Uber and said I could leave my car up here for the night.

As I waited for my ride to come, I got a call from a number I didn't recognize. I thought it was my Uber driver until I answered it and heard my mama's voice.

"Dixon!"

"Mama, how are you calling me this late?" I looked at my phone confused as hell.

"My lil guard bitch got me a phone up in here. That's not what we talking about though. Why did my woman go by my mama's house to start getting shit set up for me and the people there said you sold it?"

"I didn't know she was going by there to check on shit for you," I said the first thing that came to my mind.

"Dixon that don't matter! Bitch did you sell my mama's house?"

"Yes, mama but calm down. Listen."

"No bitch, ain't no calm down. When I get out, I'm going to hurt your trifling ass! You hear me! I'm going to kill you bitch." My mama screamed and I hung up in her face. I would deal with her and her yelling another day. There was nothing either one of us could do right now, so she needed to leave me alone and go to bed. I'm way too drunk for that shit right now.

"Dixon, I think this is your Uber out here." Paul got my attention.

I walked out to the car and when I opened the back door, I fell inside.

"Seatbelt please." The older white lady said, making me roll my eyes. I put my seatbelt on and that made me start thinking about the time Tish, Krystal, and I got kicked out of an Uber because we were all drunk and vomited in the backseat. I truly missed them so much and being drunk without them just didn't feel right. It's horrible that in under 6 months, I pushed away the two women who had my back through it all. We were like Destiny's Child back in the day. Now Beyonce was all alone.

"Can we stop and get you some coffee? Maybe a ginger ale or something?"

"No, I'm fine." I declined her offer. I now had my friends on my mind strong and with the way my life was going I could at least make it right with them.

"Actually, can we change my drop-off address to The Nationals in downtown?"

"Sure, give me the address. But just to let you know it will change your rate."

"That's fine, I'll pull the address up," I replied, then searched it on my phone to give to her.

About twenty-two minutes went by and then we pulled in front of the large Nationals sign. I gulped the lump in my throat seeing the very glass I got shot in front of. I sat there for more than ten seconds thinking if I actually wanted to go in or not.

"Ma'am, I have another ride to pick up." The driver rushed my decision.

"Okay, my bad. I'm going." I got out and tugged on the bottom of my skirt.

Once I walked up to the door, I stumbled into the lobby where an attendant was waiting just like a hotel.

"Yes ma'am, how can I assist you?"

"I need to go up to my friend's apartment to talk to her." I slurred my words.

"Okay, who is your friend, and are you on the list?"

"No, she didn't know I was coming."

"Well, I'm sorry ma'am. We only allow entrance to those who know the access codes or are on the list?"

"How do you know I don't know the access code?"

"Do you? If so, you can go type it into that elevator and make your way up." She gave me a nice nasty smile.

I rolled my eyes and then walked back to the front door to step outside and call Tish. The phone rang more than four times before Tish finally answered the phone. I missed her voice.

"Hello?"

"Hey, I'm so happy you answered Tish. It's me, Dixon."

"I know who this is Dixon." She sighed heavily.

"Listen, I'm downstairs and I was wondering if you could give me permission to come up."

"Downstairs? At my place."

"Yes."

"Dixon it's late, I'm in bed."

"I know but I can't go to sleep tonight until I talk to you. I need to talk to my friend tonight. Is that so bad Tish?" I pleaded, only this vulnerable because of the liquor.

"It's not bad Dixon, but I wish you would've picked a better time to come. Look, I'll come downstairs and talk to you for a few minutes. I guess I'll leave Noelle here with her uncle since her dad isn't home yet."

"Okay cool, thank you."

Tish hung up the phone and I sat down on the sofa in the corner, looking away from my past crime scene. Once the elevator opened, Tish climbed off in a long Hot pink sundress with her arms crossed.

"Thank you for coming down." I greeted her with a smile.

"First off, how are you?"

"I'm as good as I can be."

"Yeah, me too," I responded before a brief moment of silence.

"Anyway, I was just coming to apologize to you for ever making you feel like I wasn't a good friend or a good person. I love you like a sister, and my actions weren't justified but I hope they will be one day. Someone suggested I go to therapy and I'm really considering it now. I think it will help me be a better person."

I rambled as Tish switched the weight on her foot.

"Dixon, are you drunk? Did you drive over here?"

"No, I took an Uber because I had to come talk to you. I'm back in Dallas for good now."

"Oh. Are you and Keys moving down here?"

"No." I dropped my head.

"Keys and I are not together anymore. He was a dog, and he wasn't who I thought he was."

"Well, who did you think he was Dixon? I mean that's what happens when you marry someone you don't know." She caught a quick attitude with me. I could tell by the way she was looking at me with narrowed eyes that she was still in her feelings. I had to drop my pride for her though. She gets a pass tonight to say whatever she wants.

"I know, I didn't know him, but I was just hoping he was a good person."

"Yeah. Well, I was hoping you were a good person too."

"I am Tish, you know me. I'm broken, I do crazy shit all the time."

"And I'm broken too Dixon, but you don't see me out here backstabbing my friends! I can't trust you anymore. And without trust I can still have love for you, but I can't have you around my family." she crushed me, with that reply.

"Tish you're saying that as if I would hurt y'all. If anything, I want to protect you and who you love! That's why me and Keys broke up! Because I wanted to protect you!"

"Protect me how?" Tish asked, as her eyes glossed over and her lip quivered. The way she looked; I knew she was done with me until I proved myself loyal to her again. I can't believe I didn't say something sooner. I chose a measly seven million dollars over a lifelong allegiance with someone connected to billions. I was so stupid at first but not anymore. It's time for me to come clean.

"Tish, the other day, I saw a message in Keys phone from someone named Shadow. Upon investigation, I found out he's who kidnapped you."

"What?" Her eyes almost popped out of her skull.

"Yes, and when I asked Keys about it, he said he tipped the Shadow dude off about y'all because he owes him money and he knew Chill would come off millions for you."

"What, I, I, I don't understand."

"Me either but I had to come and tell you. Tish your friendship means more to me than any marriage. I love you and Noelle and I never want to see y'all get hurt. Especially because of a snake in y'all grass that you don't know about." Tish just stared at me in a shocked daze. She looked to be in disbelief.

Though I lied about the timeline, I still told her the truth and that's all that matters. I hope this counts for something in her heart. I honestly feel relieved now that I've gotten it off of my chest.

"Wow, I don't know what to say, Dixon."

Tish stood there panting for a minute until she walked to sit on the couch in the corner. I followed her and sat right beside her, wrapping my arm around her back.

"I have to call Chill; he needs to know." She dialed his number and held it up to her ear.

The phone rang and rang, and my stomach was in knots.

"Oh, my goodness, why isn't he answering." She got frustrated dialing his number yet again. The longer it took to hear Chill's reaction the more nervous I got. Did I make a mistake by telling her and worst of all was Keys right about Chill killing me too? I sure as hell hope not and I pray I didn't just sign my death certificate.

Chapter 13

Krystal

After Chill texted me yesterday saying he handled Ashanti I felt much better. My chest finally didn't feel as tight, and my shoulders could finally relax.

"Krys, where is your strainer?" My mama asked from the kitchen nearby. She'd invited herself over as she does from time to time to cook one of my favorite meals. It was broccoli and chicken pasta. Nobody in this world could make broccoli taste like my mama.

"Look under the cabinet by the fridge," I yelled back to her.

"No, not in there."

"Well, try the cabinet above the microwave." I listened to see if it was there.

"Thank God, finally. I can't believe you don't know your own kitchen."

"I do!"

"Huh?" She yelled and I finally got up to join her in the kitchen.

"I said I do know my kitchen; it's just been a while since I cooked."

"Well, you really shouldn't have stopped doing that baby. Home-cooked meals are more for the soul than the body. I've told you time and time again to take care of your soul first. Forget having a big booty."

"And I am, mama. I'm trying to, at least. It's just pointless to cook full-course meals because the kids only want McDonald's. I would be wasting food and money."

"Yeah, I guess I get that." She pinched my cheek.

"But as long as you're eating, I'm okay. We can't have you running around here skinny like you were in high school."

"Yes, my high school skinny was ridiculous. Child protective services should've been called on you." She and I both laughed.

I left the kitchen and went up to my bedroom to run a nice warm bath.

I got in the tub filled with Dr. Teal's salt and the last few rose petals I had left under my cabinet. After Leon and I used some on our anniversary I decided to keep the others for a special occasion. Now I'm sure there won't be another special occasion here for a while. My free time right now will be spent healing myself and looking for another job.

Just because I was going to heal myself mentally didn't mean I didn't have sexual urges. Leon may have not been the best in bed, but we had a very consistent sex life. I'm seeing now that mediocre dick is better than no dick at all.

It was quiet up here and no kids in my ear, so I decided to go grab 'Rosequan' as me and Dixon called our toys. I didn't use it often, shit the last time me and Leon pulled it out he was finished in about five minutes and Rosequan is who made me cum.

When using my toy in the tub I didn't need porn or none of that to get me off. I just closed my eyes and pictured getting the best head in the world. When I pressed the rose against my pussy the tongue-flicking sensation instantly stimulated my clit. My legs automatically spread, and my pussy instantly ooze juices into the water. My toes were curled over and I was just about to cum when my door burst open.

"Krystal!" My mom shouted and my ass quickly stood with my rose still vibrating in my hand.

"You're using that in the tub Krystal? You're going to electrocute yourself!" My mama's green ass complained.

"What mama! What is it?"

"The police are downstairs. They said they were looking for the wife of Leon Jones. You better come now Krys." She quickly left back out of the restroom.

My heart instantly dropped, and I hurried to put on my clothes to rush down the stairs. When I saw the cop's face, I knew it was something bad.

"Yes, officers?"

"Are you the wife of Leon Jones?"

"Yes, I am." They both looked at one another before the one on the right began to speak.

"Mrs. Jones. We regret to inform you that your husband was found deceased two days ago. I am so sorry to be delivering this news." He finished, and I fell back into my mother's arms. No matter how much I hated Leon I never wanted to see him dead. My kids were going to be heartbroken.

"Do you know what happened to him?" I asked while me and my mama embraced each other.

"We can not say at the moment, but the medical examiner will find out with more extensive examinations."

Even though I asked that question I was still thinking that maybe this all goes back to that night I blacked out. Had I really killed Leon and Nick covered up for me? If that's the case this would all make sense. Leon has most likely been dead since the night we fought, and I will be going to jail when they find out.

Chapter 14

Tish

One year later

Calabasas California

This morning, I got up and started moving about my room so quickly because I wanted everything to be perfect. My friends were coming to California for the first time, and I was super excited for their visit. Even with all the money in the world, I was still a mommy first. Having a toddler and a four-month-old was draining so this fun was much needed.

"Okay Ace, okay Daddy. Mommy is going to get you." I spoke to my baby boy who cried from his bassinet. Anytime his daddy heard him crying he would tell him to man up but time and time again I had to remind Chill he was a baby.

"Mommy, are you up?" Noelle peaked her head in my bedroom door. Our new house was 7,000 square feet and we pretty much stayed ducked off in the corner of it. Noelle and I were used to being in smaller spaces, but Chill insisted on buying this fifty-million-dollar mansion for us anyway.

"Hey, I'm up my sweet stuff."

"Is my baby brother up?"

"Yes, he's up and he's a little cranky because mommy needs to feed him. What do you want to eat princess?"

"I already told Renee I want chocolate chip pancakes and strawberries."

"Oh, that sounds good, I didn't know she was already in the kitchen. I told her to take the morning off." I shook my head at her willingness to please others. Renee moved in with us about six months ago after we got this house. Without her, I'm sure I wouldn't have any hair left but she helped and kept me sane during this difficult time.

I popped out one of my breasts and started to feed Ace as I walked Noelle back into the kitchen.

"Good morning, Renee."

"Good morning, Tish, good morning, Acey boo." She walked over to pinch at his little red cheeks. He had Carmel skin and red cheeks surrounding the dimples he inherited from me. He had his daddy's cold black hair and Chill's defined eyebrows that always made him look serious. My little man was every bit of his father, and it broke my heart every day that Chill had yet to spend time with him.

"Tish, I was supposed to ask you last night, but I accidentally let it slip my mind. What day are we leaving for Vegas? The trial starts on what day again?"

"June 6th, it makes me nervous to even think about it."

"Me too, but I've been praying for him. He just can't go down for this. Chill is a good man. He would never kill those men in cold blood." Renee simply shook her head. I didn't reply because my opinion of Chill wasn't quite in line with hers. He would never tell me, and I would never admit to anyone, but I do think Chill would kill if he had to. If someone threatened me or Noelle, he would have no problem pulling the trigger. That's what kept me up at night because I wasn't expecting a good outcome from this trial. After all, I remember that night and the look inside Chill's eyes when he told me to leave that section with those guys. I thank God the police had no footage inside the club because had the cameras not been wiped out, I would probably be on the stand on June 6th being grilled by the prosecution.

As I breastfed my baby, I sat on the bar stool.

"Can I make you something Tish?"

"First off, you're not supposed to be in here. I gave you the morning off remember."

"I know, but I enjoy it. I love cooking for you guys." She spoke, as she poured chocolate chips into some batter.

"Well, if you insist. I'll take an egg and a bagel."

"Coming right up." She smiled, moving about the kitchen. Chocolate chip pancakes did sound good, but I decided to keep it light since I still had a pudge. Surgery wasn't an option and I planned to get back in shape naturally. Going under the knife sounded too scary to me.

For tonight, I had an extra special girdle to wear to keep up with Krystal and Dixon who both still looked great. Even Krystal's body had snapped back after having her baby a few months before me. At least it looked like she snapped back from all of the pictures and videos she posted now and again.

When the doorbell rang, I knew it was my sister because she told me she was leaving Malibu twenty-five minutes ago. She and Nick had a two-bedroom flat overlooking the beach. I was happy for the progress they made while I was still side-eyeing Nick for playing her and Krystal. Chill however convinced me to let it go and told me his brother really seems to like my sister now. I guess I could credit him two-timing her and my friend to his age and him being spoiled by Chill his entire life.

    While Renee went to open the door, I saw that my baby had completely stopped sucking my nipple which meant he was full. I tucked my breast in and held him up to burp when my sister came in talking at her ridiculous volume.

"TT, baby! Give me some love." She stopped at the door and squatted for Noelle to run up and jump in her arms.

"Ahh, he's sleeping?"

"Yes, I'm about to put him down. So be loud in another part of the house. Hey sissy." I kissed her on the cheek.

"Where are your clothes?"

"Oh, about that." She poked her lip out.

"Tasha don't tell me you're bailing on my birthday plans."

"I am but I swear I'll make it up to you. My stomach hurts."

"That's not why, I know you just don't want to be around Krystal."

"Well so. I mean no I don't want to see her but that's not why I'm not going. I'm on my cycle. I just stopped by here to see y'all."

"Mmhmm, whatever. You owe me brunch asap." I yelled at her.

I left Tasha in the other room to put Ace down in his crib. Then I went to take a shower and washed my bundles to give them a curly look. Tasha and Noelle came into the closet where I had a built-in vanity to play with her dolls as I did my makeup. It was my grand idea to put a doll house inside my closet to entertain Noelle when I was getting ready. Chill and I decided a long time ago that we didn't want an iPad kid and wanted her to grow up being active.

As I did my makeup, my phone rang from the charger and when I saw it was Chill, I hurried and accepted the charges. When I answered I went through all the steps and finally my baby said.

"Hey Mama, happy birthday." I smiled and walked out of the room to hear him better.

"Hey baby, thank you. I have been anticipating your call."

"And I have been anticipating making it. You still stepping out tonight?"

"Yes, me and the girls are hitting the streets."

"Okay, okay, but did y'all take the necessary measures to make sure y'all good?"

"Yes Chill, I have security coming with us and we are entering and leaving the club through a side entrance. They told me when Kylie Jenner came to that club, they took her through those same doors."

"Okay, I just want to make sure you're straight. I probably won't get any sleep tonight worrying about you." He got quiet and I knew there was truth in what he was saying. Chill was protective as hell when he was free but now he was like on ten with it. He hired men for their protection but he still didn't believe in loyalty after what I told him about Keys.

"I'll be fine tonight baby. I have two special babies to come home to tonight."

"You damn right. Did you get a chance to order a birthday cake?"

"Yeah, I got Buttered Pecan icing which sounded so bomb and this place has really good cakes. I'm going to take you there when you come home."

"If, I get to come home. Let's see how the trial goes." He sounded defeated which wasn't like him. When he would give me this energy, I did everything I could to speak light into him.

"Baby, there are no ifs. You are coming home and enjoying life with me and your beautiful kids. We're going to take those trips we talked about, we're going to have even more babies, and we're going to get married soon. Even if I have to propose to you myself."

I heard him chuckle which means I made him smile.

"You don't have to worry about doing that mama. Trust I'll be the one on my knee. Where are my babies? Noelle around?"

"Yeah, let me go get her." I stepped back into the closet putting the phone on speaker.

"Here she is, talk Chill."

"Hey, Daddy baby."

"Hi, Daddy!" She flashed the wide smile she inherited straight from him.

"What you doing?"

"Playing with TT."

"Oh, hey Tasha."

"Hey bro, I hope all is well," Tasha spoke into the phone.

"Daddy?"

"Yes, lil mama?"

"Why are you not here to sing happy birthday to mommy tonight?"

"I'm sorry I can't but I will sing her happy birthday on the phone."

"Okay. And daddy?"

"Yes ma'am? I'm tired of missing you."

I folded my lip over because her emotions affected me more than my own.

"I'm tired of missing you too and I wish I was there baby. I'm sorry I can't be. You know I love you right?" His voice cracked, so I knew he was getting upset.

"I love you too daddy."

"Okay, Tish, can you hear me?"

"Yes, baby?"

"Okay, I'll talk to you in the morning. My stomach hurts, I'm about to go try and lay down."

"Alright, I love you. Later."

"Love you, happy birthday and later." He hung up the phone. Life was truly unfair right now and I was ready for this nightmare to finally be over.

3 hours later

By the time Dixon and Krystal showed up at the door, I was in a robe still finding it hard to stop crying. I hadn't started my makeup because my face was so wet, and I'd been sitting in this mirror for hours unable to get it right.

When I walked into the foyer Renee had already let them in and when they saw me, they gave me an over-the-top hello from down the hall.

"Friends, I missed y'all!" I started a light jog running towards them. We all hugged each other tightly jumping around in a circle. Until Krystal got a good look at me.

"Tish, I thought you were going to be ready when we got here. I know I didn't do my makeup on the plane for nothing."

"You did it good though friend. I was impressed with your work during all that turbulence." Dixon complimented Krystal. Though their friendship was still a bit rocky, they were working on it. With all the death around us lately, we've all seen how truly short life is. They made up on Christmas Day when we all had coffee with one another. It was like pulling teeth to get them to come out but I'm glad I did.

"Can I get you ladies anything before I show you to your rooms?" Renee asked.

"No, I'm good."

"And I'm fine," Krystal spoke after Dixon.

"Okay, we'll follow me." She led them to the rooms we had set up for each one of them this weekend. In that time, I went back to my room and finished what I could in a short amount of time. We at least needed to leave here by 9:00 so that meant I had forty-five more minutes to make myself look like something. As I sat at my vanity once more, I looked in the mirror and spotted Chill's favorite jacket hanging up behind me. Little things like that and reminders of him made me think of him even more.

I put on my eyelashes and grabbed my powder to finish my face but by that time I already had another tear running.

"Fuck!

"Fuck!"

I yelled, hitting my desk with a closed fist. I started to cry so hard my tears went silent until I gasped loudly to breathe.

"Best friend, you okay in here?" I heard Krystal's voice coming through my room. I didn't respond and when she walked in, she quickly saw that I was in fact not okay.

"Tish, what's wrong baby?" She rushed over to me.

"I'm sorry, I'm sorry but this is just so hard."

"What? Doing your makeup? I'll help you." She grabbed my foundation from my hand.

"No, not my makeup, just life. Life is so hard Krys and I know you know that. I'm sorry for not being strong but I'm not strong like you are." I placed my head on her shoulder.

"Is it Chill's situation that has you upset?"

I just nodded my head yes and she embraced me tightly.

"It's okay, everything is going to be okay. Chill will be home in no time."

"But will he Krystal? What if he's not? What if they give him life and I'm stuck out here alone? Then none of this will mean anything. All of this money and this big ass house can't replace the way that man makes me feel. No amount of money can replace him. If things don't go right in two weeks, I don't know what I will do. I don't know how I'll explain to Noelle that her daddy's never coming home."

"Yes, it's hard, trust me it's so so hard but you will find the strength to do it. You're just as strong as me Tish. You've been through so much and you still hold yourself together with dignity. Give yourself more credit." She held me up by my shoulders to look me in my face.

"I'm trying Krystal, I'm trying so hard."

"And you're doing it! Look at the both of us. New babies, being single mothers and we're surviving!" Krystal finished just as Dixon and Noelle came into the room.

"What's wrong?" Dixon questioned as she put Noelle down from her arms.

"Mommy, are you crying?" Noelle ran over to me.

"She's upset about C-H-I-L-L." Krystal tried to speak in code.

"I know you just spelled my daddy's name." Noelle spat, and that brought a much-needed grin to my face. She was too smart for her own good.

"Aww, well I'm sorry you're having a bad day." Dixon pouted her lips.

"No, I'm sorry. Y'all came out here for a good time and I'm in here being a drama queen. I'm going to get it together I swear."

"But you honestly don't have to be friend. How about we just stay in tonight and catch up with one another and watch some T.V. Does that sound better to you?"

"I'm down for that. I could use girl talk. You Tish?"

I nodded my head yes as I wiped a tissue under each eye. Staying in with loved ones was what I needed on my birthday since I couldn't spend it with the man I loved. This can't be life now."

Chapter 15

Chill

The next morning

When I first came to prison, I used to rush to the phone to call Tish and see how they were doing. Now calling was just a harsh reminder that I was locked up and away from the ones I love. I barely got any sleep last night and I sat up thinking about my life as a whole. Would I be here if I didn't make so much money? Did I get cocky in sloppy once I hit billionaire status?

I often told myself I did because I was pulling the trigger left and right, looking in niggas eyes when I took their life. Now I have to wonder was any life I took worth losing mine too? Nah, to be honest, it wasn't. Not one person was worth me spending my life behind bars except niggas like Shadow.

The niggas I killed at the club sure as hell wasn't because I should've kicked them out and been done with it. Now I got all their families ready to prosecute me and take me away from my family for good.

"Saint, you have a visitor." A guard knocked on my cell door before it buzzed and opened. Usually, it was my lawyers who came to see me, but I finally decided to let other people come. People that I've been needing to see for some time now. I couldn't have this conversation I'm about to have in a letter, so it had to be had face to face. Real men face their opps head-on, especially when it used to be your homie.

"Chill, my smooth Patna." Keys spoke after I lifted the phone to my ear. He was coming into this situation blind, and I was waiting to see how he would react. To be honest, this conversation was long overdue, and I couldn't sit and wonder for any longer, I may be sitting and wondering for the rest of my life if that's the case.

"Talk to me man, anything I need to know."

"Shid, nothing new besides my lil clothing shop is taking off in Chicago. Everyone wants that Killer Swagg, apparel." He smiled, giddy in his seat.

"Anything I need to know about the streets? My family good right?"

"Of course. I've been looking after them as much as I can from where I am. I wish I could move where they are, but you know duty in Chicago calls."

"Understood."

"Stella ass pregnant again. Don't even ask me how because I still don't know." He laughed, looking shocked when I didn't join in.

"But are you good bruh? The weight of everything wearing down on you?"

"To be honest with you yeah it is. The trial coming up, I've been in here for over a year, and I've been battling with the thoughts of my best friend snaking me."

He sat up in his seat much less relaxed than before.

"Who snaked you bruh?"

"You did."

"Me? Nah, nah, I don't snake shit. You know I wouldn't do you like that."

"Be quiet bruh, it's my time to talk because you've been running your mouth for too long."

He knew to shut the fuck up.

"Now, Shadow had someone he let in on his plan with you who told me a few things in a letter. You and I both know what they are. So tell me I'm a dumb ass nigga for believing it because I want to feel like a dumb ass nigga more now than at any other time in my life bruh. Tell me this shit ain't true." I got closer to the glass. I didn't tell him where the info came from because I didn't want him to kill Dixon.

"Chill, man I don't know what to say."

"Nigga, the truth now or you won't get a chance to lie to me anymore later."

He shook his head profusely as he bit his lip.

"Alright, first off bruh you know I love you like a real brother. I'm talking blood couldn't make us any closer."

"Get to the point."

"Shadow contacted me about the money I owed him from that little stickup. I didn't have it and I didn't know what to do when he killed my cousin and threatened the rest of my family."

"So it is true. You threw my family in the line of danger to save yours."

"It's not like that, he was never going to actually hurt them, and I made sure of that?"

"You were with him at the warehouse where he had them?"

"Chill listen."

I took the phone away from my ear for a few seconds to keep from saying the wrong thing. Keys just sat with his head down unable to look me in my eyes at this point.

"Keys, look at me like a man nigga. Why didn't you come to me? Why risk the person you know means the world to me for your own personal gain? Gangsta shit aside bruh that hurt. I would've made shit work for you?"

"Would you Chill, or would you have shut me out? You always shut me out and tell me my troubles aren't valid enough for your time. Had I come to you, you would've brushed it off and made me lose people who mean the world to me. Just imagine if you were in my exact same position dealing with what I'm going through. You would risk whatever to save your family."

He was finally being real with me at this point.

"Keys I see you clueless when it comes to my loyalty, and I don't know if it is my fault or yours. Nigga I wouldn't have slept until Shadow was where he is now for fucking with your family."

"And I didn't know that, at least I didn't feel that way. I feel bad about it. I couldn't breathe while they were with him, but I know Shadow and he doesn't kill women and kids. He is not as grimy as we are. He's never been that nigga, he a thief but he not cold-hearted."

"I guess not."

I respond and he nervously tapped his fingers hanging on for my next word. I didn't know what to say, and to be honest I didn't know what to feel.

"So, I guess there is nothing I could do to prove my loyalty to you huh?"

"I ain't say that. Who knows where life will bring us? Do I think I ever trust you around my family? Hell nah. But time will tell. We will see what will happen if I ever get out of here."

"You will bruh, I will make sure of it. I have been praying about it." He replied and my eyes shot open wider hearing the code words.

I have been praying about it; meant he was laying low on a witness or somebody else harmful to me. My guess is that he's located the rat ass nigga Concord who is the prosecution's star witness in my trial. Word got to me that they caught him up on a drug charge and offered him immunity to testify against me.

"Well, if you been praying about it then hopefully your prayer will come true."

"It definitely will. You gotta be free, the free world needs you."

He replied, and I simply shook my head, okay. Without saying another word to Keys I hung up the phone and made my way back to my cell. This could all be my new reality after trial.

Let's see if Keys's guilt really fuels him to get me out of this shit. If he does, then maybe I might just learn to forgive him.

Chapter 16

Nick

"I was wondering when you would get here. I saw you were stuck in traffic when I checked your location."

Tasha said, climbing into my car to go to a club in Hollywood.

"Yeah, you know traffic a bitch out here. You look like you taste good."

"As do you. I missed you today," she leaned over the seat putting her sticky lipgloss over my lips.

Tasha had this rule where we always had to have a date night at least once every two weeks to make sure we made time for each other. With me opening up this dispensary in Inglewood, I was busy most of the day. At night I tried to give her all of my attention, but it was hard when I was excited about something else.

Driving around Cali was always a vibe because we rode with the windows down and enjoyed the palm trees sprouted everywhere. I can't wait until my brother gets out and we can take over the city. Just like Chicago and Vegas, L.A. would be ours one day too.

Once we parked and walked up to the club entrance, we stood outside in line for only a few minutes before I decided to throw my weight around.

"Come on, let's go," I told Tasha as I stepped up to the security guard at the front of the line. He acted like he didn't see me at first until I looked him up and down.

"Can I do something for you homie?"

"Yeah, I'm Nick Saint. CEO of Saint ENT." I stuck my hand out in front of him.

"The CEO of Saint ENT is Chill Saint. Nice try though." He turned his back to me.

"Chill isn't acting CEO as of now because he's out of commission. So that means you talking to the man who owns the most famous nightclub in the world. Show me some respect or I'll make sure that line behind us disappears within the next week."

"Well, what can I do for you, sir?"

"Move out the way and let us in. Simple." I ordered and he stepped to the side.

"Did you just do that?" Tasha grabbed my arm to stop me from behind.

"Yeah, I'm not playing with these niggas. They are about to start respecting me just as they do Chill." I replied, and she gave me a devilish grin.

"Fuck, I want to suck your dick right now."

"Well let's go to our table, they got tablecloths in here," I responded, and she started to smile even harder. We went to our booth in the corner, Tasha dropped down under the table, and within seconds she had my dick out of my pants.

"Hello." A waiter approached us just as I could feel my tip at the back of Tasha's throat.

"I'll be your waiter today. Can I start you off with any beverages?" He asked, and it was honestly hard to talk.

"Let me, let me get a water, two waters."

"Okay, anything else like an appetizer. I would recommend the cheese fries."

"Nah, that's it." I shooed her away from the table. Tasha kept sucking my dick so powerfully, I bust a load into the back of her throat pressing my teeth in my lips. She came up from under the table smiling and I used the napkin to wipe my semen off the side of her lips.

"Thank you, darling."

"No, thank you. With yo fine ass." I made her smile.

"I can't believe I just did that. I liked it though. Imma do it again."

"Give me like twenty minutes. I feel dizzy."

I made her laugh. That's honestly all she ever did around me. If she wasn't laughing, she was cooking, and when she wasn't cooking, we were having sex. I had the perfect life with her. She was really my soul mate and I honestly felt like I loved her ass.

Tasha and I ordered our food, and it came out pretty quickly. I was high and had the munchies, so I tore my shit up, but I had to check with lil picky. She didn't like any of the food we ate in Cali.

"Did you like it?"

"Yeah, it was good. I make a better steak than this though."

"Why did I know that was coming." She smiled at me before she said, "Whatever." and looked back at her phone. She rolled her eyes so hard at the screen her irritation caught my attention.

"What's wrong with you?"

"Nothing."

"So, we lying to each other now?" I raised my eyebrow.

"It's nothing really, it's just that bitch Krystal is here, and I still don't want to see her."

"She with Tish?"

"Yes, and she will be here the whole weekend so I can't go over my own sister's house. When she came last night, I left."

"Why though? You told me y'all we're cool. Are you like this now because of our past?"

"Yes, because of y'all past. I don't want to be friends with someone who I was unknowingly sharing dick with." She tore up her face.

"Tasha."

"What? Would you hang out with a man you know I fucked with?"

"Nah, and watch your mouth,"

"See, you would feel the same way I feel. That's Tish's friend. We don't have to speak." She downed the glass of champagne she poured.

"Stop Tasha. You forgave me so you need to let that shit go. Y'all better than this. And I told you had I knew y'all were close like that, I wouldn't have been fucking her. You see who I chose." I reached out and grabbed her hand.

"I know, and that's why the bitch stopped talking to me. She doesn't like shit on social media anymore. She doesn't call me; she doesn't send those motivational or holiday messages like she used to. So, fuck her. She needs to be at home taking care of that baby she just had instead of traveling."

Tasha aggressively ripped into a dinner roll after telling me some information I didn't know. While Tasha finished the last of the wine in the bottle, I pulled out my phone and went to Krystal's Instagram page for the first time in almost a year. There weren't many updates but there was a baby announcement with a little foot next to a sign that said four months old. When I did the math that could very much be my child. Now I had to look into this shit and reach out to an old acquaintance.

Chapter 17

Dixon

One week later

"Bye y'all, I'll see everyone in two days."

I waved as I left out of the clinic. I loved my new job and position because the hours here were nothing like the hospital. I was able to clock in and out at a certain time and have enough time to go home to my man.

While Chance was in town, I made sure to spend every hour I could with him. We did sculpting, we ran in the park, and we made sure to go to church faithfully every Sunday. I was excited about tonight because for the first time, Chance was flying me to an undisclosed location. Though small planes gave me anxiety, I trusted the pilot with my life.

I also had a little pep in my step because I got a letter from my mama this morning saying she had been caught sleeping with that guard and they added even more time to sentence. They'd already stopped her release last year because they found that cell phone she had. I felt bad being happy, but I was because my life was peaceful, and she just would've interfered with that getting out any time soon.

When I walked into my apartment, I put all of my things on the counter and took off my tennis shoes. As soon as I walked into the living room, I jumped out of my skin seeing Keys sitting on my sofa. This was a face I hadn't saw in person in a long time and his presence seemed to have a gloomy ora over it. When he stood up, I started to scream, and he came towards me, grabbing me at my waist.

"Chill, I'm not going to hurt you. Just relax. I came here to talk to you."

"Keys how did you get in my apartment? You have no right to be here. We are not together." I threw my elbows hoping to get free from his hold.

"When did we get a divorce? I don't remember that happening. You just left Vegas and felt like we were over."

"Yeah, and I've been too busy trying to move on to think about you or a divorce. You need to go. We have nothing to talk about."

"Yes, we do. I came down here to have a conversation with you. It's been too long. I miss you; I think about you a lot."

He moved his even longer dreads out of his face. He was still fine as hell but with a smaller frame than before. He looked like he'd lost a lot of stress weight since I last saw him. That's what happens when you have a worrisome ass baby mama like Stella.

"Don't you and your bitch have a baby on the way?"

"Oh, so you have been keeping up with me huh?" He smirked as if that meant I still cared. I mean I didn't, I only checked his page because I wanted to be nosy but nothing more than that. I used to check it faithfully a while ago but now I only look maybe once every few weeks. I was truly moved on, and happy with my new man.

"Whatever Keys. As I said, you should go. I don't want you here."

"I understand that. But I just wanted to let you know I'm thankful for you for everything you did for me. Telling them to operate on me, taking care of me, never telling Chill our secret."

He made my heart skip a beat.

"And just to let you know it's out in the open now because one of Shadow's people told him. We talked about it, and I think we will be straight eventually."

"Yeah, well I'm happy for y'all. I hope everything works out for you and your family."

"But you are my family too. Look I know the first time we got together it wasn't by choice and neither one of us remembers it. We started off on some rocky ass terms, so we were destined to fail. But this time, I want it to be different."

"It can't be different Keys. How can we just erase everything that happened between us? You just show up here at my house as if we aren't already over. I've moved on from you and the thought of us being together. I deserve better and I deserve someone who's pure, and good, and kind."

"Oh, so someone like the pilot you been posting about. Yeah, I've come to your page a few times recently and saw him."

"Well then you should've seen that I'm happy with him, so I don't need you in my life anymore."

"So you choosing that broke-ass glorified bus driver over me." I rolled my eyes so hard it physically hurt my sockets.

"Keys, Chance is a pilot, he does not drive a bus."

"Plane, greyhound, same thing. He will never have as much money as me. Pilots have to fly planes for fifty years before they can retire."

"Well in fifty years we will be able to travel the world if the lord says the same. Look you need to go." I walked to the door and opened it as he stood there shaking his head.

"Alright." He shrugged his shoulder before walking to the front door.

"We will see how long y'all last."

"We will as long as God says the same."

He started to laugh.

"What's so funny."

"Nothing, just the fact that you think I'm going to just let you be happy and I want you back."

"Why do you want me back all of a sudden? Keys I haven't heard from you in a year!"

"Because I realized what we had. I let my baby mama pull us apart when she got out of jail, but I should've stood my ground with her. Look me coming down here to visit Chill made me think of you."

"Well, you can clear your mind of me because I'm with someone now."

"So, fuck him."

"No Keys, fuck you." He put both of his hands in his pockets.

"Alright, be that way and enjoy your Airbus driver while you can."

"And what does that mean?"

"As I said, enjoy him while you can. You'll be running back to me once he's gone, and yo pretty ass want to be dipped in gold again." He rubbed his thumb across my lip before he walked out of my front door.

"I'll talk to you again soon Dix."

"I highly doubt that."

I slammed the door and locked both locks behind him. I immediately got on the phone with a locksmith because I wanted my locks changed today. Keys was losing his damn mind, but he better go make it work with his baby mama because I've grown too much and become too happy to go backward.

After I looked out my bedroom window a million times, I was finally convinced Keys was gone. I got in the shower, washed my body in my favorite soap, and did my makeup nice. I felt like tonight would be the night I finally broke Chance and slept with him. Though he was celibate, we bonded on a higher level, but that still didn't stop my urges.

Once I got dressed and did my makeup along with my hair, I was finally ready. Grabbing my to-go bag, I left out of my house with plans of not coming home for a couple of days. Chance told me to meet him at the Strout airport in south Dallas to take off. I put on my favorite R&B jams and glided to the location.

When I made it to the runway, I saw the tiny airplane up ahead and my stomach started to hurt. It however eased up when I saw Chance standing there in his pilot uniform. I know it wasn't necessary for tonight, but he knew I loved to see him in it. This man always thought of any way he could make me happy.

When I parked and got out, I ran up to him in my six-inch heels jumping in his arms. When I went to kiss him, he moved his head back and put me down on the ground.

"Babe?" I questioned him, seeing a very uncomfortable look on his face.

"Are you okay?"

"No, I'm not actually." He looked at me with so much disappointment my heart started to beat faster.

"What happened?"

"I got this on my way here, via my Facebook account." He lifted his phone to my face and played a video of me getting fucked from the back. When I looked at it closely, I saw it was none other than Keys behind me giving me long strokes.

"Baby, I can explain, that video is old. That's not recent."

"Dixon, that doesn't matter. I got the video and now this image is embedded in my mind. I can't marry someone with videos circulating like this. Especially when I saw it."

"Marry someone?" I held on to the last part I heard.

"Yes marry, I wanted to marry you. That's why I planned all this. I was going to fly us to a private island and propose to you there."

"Okay, Chance, we can still get married baby. Don't judge me from this one video."

"I'm not judging you, Dixon. I'm just paying attention to the red flags when they show themselves. Look, my ex-wife used to take videos of herself sleeping with other men too. I saw some of them, and this is just a sore reminder that maybe I shouldn't be getting married."

"Chance."

"Dixon, I'm sorry but I can't do it. Take care of yourself." He turned and climbed into the cockpit of the plane before shutting the door. When he cranked the engine, the wind started whipping so fast, that dust and gravel flew towards my face. I then backed off the runway, coughing as he prepared to take off. Just as quickly as Chance came into my life, he was leaving because of the man I never should've married in the first place.

Chapter 18

Krystal

Once my work shift at the daycare was over, my feet were screaming for a seat. This was my third month working here and I was enjoying it thus far. I didn't tell my parents the details of me losing my job, and simply said I was tired of teaching. My mama was happy to have me working side by side with her and paid me enough money to take care of myself along with Leon's social security check I got for the kids.

"Okay, mama. I'm gone. Kids, be good for grandma, okay? Charlotte, tell grandma she was wrong for not inviting you to the sleepover."

"Unt unt. Don't turn my youngest baby against me. I will be getting her next weekend when I don't have Madagascar one and two." She referred to my other kids.

"Mama don't do my babies. They getting better."

"Yeah, better." She smiled because she knew she loved them. We'd all tried to not be so hard on them after they found out their daddy died. My only mistake in how I handled that situation was not telling them sooner. I sat them down on the morning of the funeral and I think they were both in shock the entire service.

After Leon died it seemed like my life did a complete switch out of nowhere. Everything in the world seemed different and for the first time in many years, I didn't have a man on my side. I was however okay with it and finding my way one day at a time. I now had three babies on my own but a village to help take care of them all.

I walked out of the daycare center and to my car when I heard my name being called.

"Krystal."

I heard from behind me. I knew exactly who it was because was so hard to forget the scent that was being carried in the wind.

"Nick, what are you doing here?"

"It was hard to get in touch with you. I mean you did block me on everything."

"Yeah, I did and for a good reason too. Excuse me." I opened up my car door to place Charlotte in the backseat.

"I know how you feel about me, but I made this trip here because I needed to talk to you."

"About?"

"The baby."

"What baby?"

"The baby you have right here." He pointed at Charlotte's car seat.

"Okay, what about her?"

"I want to know if she is mine?"

"No, she's not."

"You hate me that bad that you would keep my first child away from me?"

"No, Nick!" I quickly got irritated.

"Nick, I love my freedom and I want to keep it so I can take care of my kids."

"Your freedom? What the fuck are you talking about?"

I slammed the door making Charlotte start to whine.

"Nick, you know what happened with Leon and you know we were responsible. He never left that night. You found him dead and got rid of him for me. You can stop being dishonest with me!"

"Okay and?"

"Nick, you lied to me, and I believed you. Thank goodness the cops have yet to trace that back to us."

"And they won't."

"And they will as soon as they find out I was having an affair with you and got pregnant with your child."

Nick started to slowly bob his head up and down.

"So, she is mine."

"Of course, she's yours Nick but no one can know that. As soon as clues start to fall people will put together their own stories about us and my kids and our daughter will never have either of us. You have to know that."

I was dead set on how I felt because I thought about the different outcomes of our affair and what we would be up against in court. I would rather raise Charlotte on my own with no discussion than have to ever explain Nick and my relationship. The few people that knew will be the only people that will ever know.

"So, what Krystal? I'm supposed to just walk away and pretend like my kid isn't here."

"Yeah, I mean you can have one with Tasha, aren't you two in love." I crossed my arms because that situation still made me uncomfortable.

"That's irrelevant. I want to know her too Krystal. Can't I just know her? I don't have to post her; I don't have to tell people she's mine."

"No Nick! If you care anything about her you would let us be. Go back to California and live your best life with your girlfriend. We can never be anything more."

"No, we can't but I'm not giving up on her. Now I don't know what we going to do or how we going to do it but I'm going to know my daughter. If we have to ship her across state like Chill and Tish did for years, then that's what we're going to do. I'd rather be in jail than a deadbeat father. So let your paranoia go and open this door so I can see my kid before I get mad in this bitch." Nick seemed to be trying to put his foot down and he had a combative look in his eye like he was ready for war.

"Krystal, I'm tired of waiting so open the door. Now." He demanded for the second time, so I opened the car door. When he pulled the blanket from over her face that look in his eye was love at first sight.

"Yeah, your mama is going to have to call the National Guard to keep you away from me." He held her and bounced her in his arms. I'm sure now I had no choice but to try and make it work. I just had to pray to God that our brief affair and the murder of Leon would never get out.

Chapter 19

Tish

I hated to be back in Vegas under these circumstances, but I wanted to support my man. Today was the last day of trial and time for the prosecution to pull out all their major stops.

When Tasha, Nick, and I walked into the courtroom my eyes instantly went on Chill. He had a charcoal grey suit on and his favorite gold Cartier glasses. I'd dropped off everything for him to wear with his lawyer just yesterday. Everything looked better on him than I imagined.

When we went to sit down behind Chill he looked back over his shoulder and smiled at me.

"Hey, baby." I mouthed and waved at him blowing a kiss.

"Disgusting!" Someone who sat with the victim's family said. They'd been giving us evil eyes for days, but I held my head high.

"All rise." The bailiff announced and then entered the judge. The court proceedings started and the prosecution was told to call their last witness to the stand.

"The prosecution would like to call Concord Jefferson to the stand."

Everyone in the courtroom turned looking over their shoulders to see who he was. When the large six-foot-two man walked up to the stand, I was a little intimidated by his stature. Chill however didn't seem to be, and his eyes followed him the whole way. If Chill's looks could kill, that nigga would be dead right now.

Once he was sworn in, the prosecutor started asking him basic questions to start the examination.

"How long had you been working for Malachi Saint before his arrest?"

"Six years." His deep voice answered.

"Okay, and over the course of six years would you say Mr. Saint was a good boss."

"Yeah, for the most part. It was easy work."

"Sounds good, now, I understand it was easy work, but can you tell me more about your job duties there?" The prosecutor paced back and forth in front of the stand.

"My duties were to secure the nightclub and make sure everything ran smoothly from open to close."

"Yeah, and by smoothly you mean no fights, contraband, or anything else that's harmful to the business, right?"

"Correct."

"Now tell me this, when something would happen against company policy, what was the protocol for handling it?"

"I'm not sure what you mean."

"Let's say if someone did something against company policy, we're you were instructed to report it to Mr. Saint?"

"Sometimes."

"And when it was, did Mr. Saint become angry or irate."

"Yeah, it's his business and he was sensitive about it."

"Was he so sensitive to where he would lash out if someone visited his club and broke the rules?

"Lash out meaning what?"

Concord asked, and the prosecutor went over to his table grabbing photos.

"Lash out meaning putting a bullet wound in these three men's heads and asking his staff to dispose of them." He held up the photos and flashed each one of them to the jury.

"Mr. Jefferson, is this the type of anger we would see come from Mr. Saint."

He asked, and I watched as Chill adjusted himself in his seat. I could tell he was starting to get uncomfortable with the questioning which was making me nervous.

"Mr, Jefferson. Can you answer my question for the courtroom? Would Mr. Saint shoot these three men and ask you to dispose of them if they broke the rules in his nightclub?"

He made me have a flashback to my first night there. My stomach turned in knots thinking about the truths of that night. Deep down inside I knew Chill did it. I remember those guys and I knew this was all my fault.

"We don't have all day for an answer Mr. Jefferson." You could see the prosecutor start to get antsy the longer it took for Concord to speak.

"No."

"I beg you pardon?"

"No, he wouldn't have." The courtroom gasped because Concord was not a witness for the defense.

"Excuse me?"

"I said he wasn't that type of boss to do no shit like that. Chill, I'm sorry, Malachi took no shit in the club, but he wouldn't have done that. He never once asked me or any of the employees to do anything illegal while working for him and that's the truth. Working with Malachi Saint, I was never told to do anything illegal and how those bodies ended up in his crematory I don't know. We did lose a pair of keys to that building a few summers ago. There's no telling who had access besides us."

The prosecutor was perplexed and tapped his fingers on the stand before saying.

"No further questions your honor."

I could tell by how red his face was that Concord's testimony wasn't good for his case which means it was awesome for us. I'm glad that he decided to hold back on the stand because he was the reason my man has been in jail this long. I wonder what gave him a change of heart.

Once both lawyers made their closing arguments, I walked up close to Chill to say goodbye.

"I'll see you later mama. I love you."

"I love you more," I replied before they took him through those back doors. When we turned to walk out of the courtroom, I stopped in my tracks seeing Keys standing near the door.

"Don't worry about him, you good I promise." Nick linked arms with me. We walked past Keys and I swear I felt a dark spirit over my body.

"Tish, can I talk to you." Keys asked, reaching for my hand.

"Hell, nah bruh, leave her alone. Can't you see she not fucking with you?"

"Man, I just wanted to apologize in person. Tell you nothing is how it may seem." He made me stop and speak up for myself and my child.

"How is it not? Look I have nothing to say to you. I don't want to be around you. No matter what you did or why you did it you still put me and my daughter's life in jeopardy. My baby still has nightmares about that night." I pushed two fingers into his chest making his shoulder jerk back.

"And that makes me feel like shit Tish but I'm doing everything I can to make up for it. I've talked to Chill. I'm trying to talk to you, and I'm making sure he comes home to you when the jury comes back with a verdict."

"How?" I asked with my forehead wrinkled and my nose scrunched up tightly.

"Why do you think Concord got on the stand and lied? It's because I had my boys back." He smiled as if he'd done the best thing in the world.

"What did you do?" Nick asked before I could.

"I got eyes on his family, and I let him know that. Had he told the truth on the stand, they would've been dead before the prosecution rested their case."

"So, you're harassing another innocent family. Very fitting for you."

"Look, y'all can say what y'all want about me but all that is going to change when I continue proving how loyal I am. Now if y'all will excuse me. I'm about to go eat I'm sure the verdict will be back soon." He replied, walking away from us.

"Man, I don't like that nigga." Tasha spat as he walked away.

"Me either, and I still don't trust him. Come on y'all, let's go try to eat something ourselves. We may be back here sooner than we think." I replied, once again saying another prayer to myself. I needed good news by the end of the day.

Chapter 20

Chill

We were on our way back to the jail when they got a call to turn around. The verdict had come in and I was honestly nervous as hell. Keys had done his job by getting Concord to flip on the stand, but I could still be railroaded if the jury felt it was right.

When I got back into the courtroom, I saw my family which consisted of Tish, Nick, and Tasha, along with Keys sitting a few feet away from them. When Tish and I locked eyes, I gave her a smile hoping to ease her nerves. I know my baby was worried and I felt horrible for being the reason. Tish had given me something I hadn't felt in years, empathy.

When the judge entered the courtroom, we were all told to stand, and I swallowed the big ass lump in my throat.

"Foreman, I understand that we have a verdict." The judge directed his attention to the jury.

"Yes, we do." An older black lady stood up with a card in her hand. When she opened it, I closed my eyes.

"On count one, for the Murder of Gage Cunners, we the jury find the defendant Malachi Saint, NOT Guilty."

My lawyer squeezed my shoulder as the people in the courtroom took a collective gasp.

"For count two, the murder of Christian Sedonas, we the jury find the defendant, Not Guilty."

That was two out of three, but I still needed to hear the last one to be sure.

"For count three, the murder of Fabian Portillo, we the jury find the defendant, Not Guilty." She finished and I felt like an anchor lifted off my chest. I looked back towards my family who all had tears in their eyes and smiles on their faces.

After a long hard year, I get to see my baby girl again and most of all hold my son for the very first time.

I'm finally going home and this time to the perfect family.

3 weeks later

"Don't worry mama, I'll get him." I stopped Tish from getting out of bed because my son was crying. Since I have been home, I've tried to take all the pressure off her since I left her for a whole year. I walked to the nursery and there was my junior lying there crying with his little pacifier in his hand.

"Hey, cut that out lil man. You crying and disturbing your mama's sleep. Do you love that girl? I get it, I love that girl too."

I didn't do much baby talk with him because I wanted to raise a man. That however didn't mean I wasn't going to have a soft spot for him. Shit, just looking at him I already wanted to give him the world.

I walked through the hallways bouncing him on my shoulders as he whined a little. Eventually, he stopped and that's when I took the opportunity to peak in Noelle's room. She was still knocked out on top of her covers with her legs spread over the bed. I chuckled and closed the door because my baby needed a queen-sized bed the way she sleeps.

Once I hit the corner on the stretch to the kitchen, I stood at the glass admiring the view through my backyard. This house was truly a castle which was very fitting for my family.

"You see all of this son. It's going to all be yours one day. Well, to be honest, I want you to have way more than this. Daddy going to make sure I set you up for it." I pointed out the glass pretty much talking to myself. Ace was blowing bubbles but one day it would all make sense to him.

"There you are. I was trying to find you to give him this." Tish held up a bottle filled with breast milk. Breastfeeding him wasn't her original plan, but I showed my concern about him using formula. My little prince needed to be fed the finest he could be offered. That liquid gold from his mama would make him smart, healthy, and most importantly strong.

"Thank you, baby." We kissed before she kissed Ace on his cheek.

"You ready for tonight? The decorators and caterers should be here around noon."

"Of course, I am."

"You want me to get him?" She held her arms out.

"No, I'll feed him. You can go relax and get some breakfast."

"Okay baby, thanks." She smiled and turned to walk away. I smacked her on her ass and Ace started to cry as she walked away.

"See, my baby doesn't like you smacking his mama's booty."

"Oh, well he can get over that. I'ma be doing that for life."

We both grinned at each other. Tish continued down the hall and I stood there watching her walk away. I don't think she even knows how much I just sit back and watch her. She was the prettiest mutha fucka in the world to me.

After I fed Ace, I gave him to Renee since Tish was in the shower. I stepped into the restroom listening to her sing as I brushed my teeth. After flossing, brushing my hair, and washing my face I went to put on clothes. It felt good to be able to dress fly again. Wearing the same thing every day fucked with a nigga spirit in jail. I changed twice a day in the outside world.

After I got dressed, I tapped on the shower glass to tell Tish I was leaving.

"I'll be back mama; I have to go sign some paperwork with Nick."

"For the dispensary?"

"Yeah, I'll be back once I'm done and I pick up my homies from the airport." I lied to her but not with ill intent. I just couldn't let her know what I was really going to do. Nick, me, and Tasha were meeting at a jeweler to pick out an engagement ring.

I showed up to the jeweler and my brother and Tasha were nowhere in sight. Instead of sitting in the car, I got out and sat on the hood to enjoy the Cali breeze. I liked it out here. I felt safe, unseen, and low-key, unlike my time in Chicago and Vegas.

While sitting there enjoying the scenery, my peace was interrupted by the loud ass music and loud ass people pulling up. When I looked behind me, Tasha's ass was out the window and Nick was encouraging her to act an ass.

I shook my head and laughed to myself because I don't know who ever let these two get together. It was like watching an episode of Wild 'N Out around them. My children's auntie and uncle were wild, to say the least.

"What up bro." Nick slapped hands with me after getting out of the car.

"Aww, I can't believe what we are doing here." Tasha ran up and hugged me.

"Yeah, I can't believe y'all pulled up here acting like that. This a multi-million-dollar jewelry store."

"And we multimillion-dollar niggas! We act how the fuck we want."

"Anyway, y'all come in. I got some shit to do after this." I walked into the jewelry store ahead of them. We sat down in a little area that had couches and was decorated like a little living area. The jeweler, Adin was my Indian patna who just did some necklaces for me walked up. He had three different rings made with the ten-million-dollar budget I gave him. Now all we had to do was pick the one I liked best to give to my queen.

We studied each ring for at least twenty minutes apiece. All three rings were beautiful, but it was the oval-cut diamond ring that we all decided on. Tish wasn't a flashy person, so this was small enough, yet classy enough for a woman of her net worth. To be honest I don't think my baby even likes being rich but that's why I was going to spoil her ass even more. She will get used to it one day.

Adin got the ring boxed up for me and sent an invoice to my accountant for the payment. We left out of the shop and walked to our cars.

"Okay, so we will be at the party around 6:00. What time are you proposing?"

"Around 9:00, it has to be dark so that the candles and letters shine."

"It's going to be set up on the terrace near the water, right?" Tasha asked with bright eyes.

"Yeah, they setting it up when the party starts."

"Aww, this is going to be so pretty. I'm so happy for y'all. We will see you later. Be safe."

"Y'all too," I said before hopping in my car. Now I had to go to the airport to pick up my niggas that we're coming in from out of town.

Snoop, Jack, and Keys were waiting for me at the airport. I could've sent a car to get them, but under the circumstances, I had to pick them up myself. I pulled up in the airport pick-up area and they were standing there chopping it up until I tooted my horn.

"My nigga!" Snoopy said loudly and they all came to the car with smiles across their face. I was happy to know that they were happy I was home.

"Look at my boy, the family man. Car seats in the back and shit." Keys clowned, after opening the car door.

"My bad, put that shit in the hatchback." I popped the truck on the Porsche. They loaded up and we took off from the airport talking shit and catching up with one another.

"Jack, I hear you got a baby on the way." I looked in the rearview mirror.

"Man, I told this nigga Snoopy not to tell nobody. He knows I'm not sure if that baby is mine."

"Still nigga, it might be. But trust you won't have to worry about DNA testing or none of that. If the baby comes out black as oil, then we know it's yours." We all laughed at Snoop. I missed these niggas and most importantly I missed being around loyalty.

As I drove away from the airport, we continued shooting the shit until we got to my next destination. It was the warehouse I purchased which I'm turning into the next hottest club in the world. Club Tish. Shit just had a ring to it.

We walked inside and they all looked around the open space shooting out ideas about the renovation.

"It would be lit if you put a wrap-around balcony above the dance floor." Keys mentioned, looking at the ceiling.

"Hell yeah and put a section right in the middle of it. Hundred-thousand-dollar section. Only the elite can sit there." Jack added in his input.

"Hell yeah, shit going to be fire. What's you going to name it?"

"Club Tish."

"Tish, I like it. I can fuck with it." Snoopy slapped hands with me."

"Come on y'all."

I walked them in a little further and that's when we made it to the table, I had Adin set up before we got here.

"Yo, what's these?" Snoopy asked, rubbing his hands together. On the table were three boxes that each had a million-dollar Cuban links inside.

I walked up to the table and opened each box showcasing the necklaces inside. They all sucked their teeth and covered their mouths with closed fists starting at the diamonds.

"As y'all can see, they each have a different color diamond in the middle of the link. Snoopy this yellow one for you." I handed the box to Snoop.

"Of course, we got the black diamond in the middle for Jack black."

"For sho, for sho." He grabbed his necklace with excitement.

"And we got the last one with the red diamond in it, for the realest nigga I know. The one I trust with my whole life. Myself." I closed the last jewelry box wiping the smile off Keys face.

I reached into my waistband and pulled out my nine and pointed it at my old best friend.

"What are you doing bruh?" His voice trembled as we looked each other eye to eye.

"I had over a year to figure out what I wanted to do with you because of that situation with Shadow. I stayed up all night sometimes wondering how I would react if I got free. After you visited me and did what was needed with Concord, I battled with myself about you being a good dude. I wondered then if I could trust you."

"And you can."

"Nah, but I can't. I really can't bruh. You know Tish and I are new. I love her to death, but Noelle. That's my blood bruh, I can't believe you helped somebody take my daughter from me." I cocked the pistol.

"Okay, okay bruh I get it. I understand how you feel and if you want me out of your world, I'll leave bruh. I promise I will leave California and never come back." He begged me, as a single tear dropped down my face.

"But I want them to be safe in the whole world, not just in one state. Why you make me do it bruh? I already had to kill one partner, but I never thought I would have to kill you."

"Chill don't do this."

"I tried bruh, but I just can't get over what you did to my family. I won't be able to sleep as long as you are alive, and I loved your snake ass too."

I shot five times in his chest.

Pop pop pop pop pop.

I hit him once more in his head so he wouldn't suffer. Jack and Snoopy both looked like deer in headlights because I hadn't told a soul what he did to me. After I wiped my hand across my face, I let my emotions go and got straight to business with them.

"Imma keep it simple like this. Y'all got necklaces tonight and Keys got bullets. As long as y'all stay loyal you won't ever get a gift like him. Now let's wrap this nigga up and prepare him to be dumped in the ocean. Come on, we don't have much time. I have a party to get to."

I finished before I stepped over the body of my old best friend.

Chapter 21

Tish

Dixon, Krystal, Tasha, and I sat at the bar set up by the pool. Though Tasha and Krystal didn't necessarily care for one another, Tasha told me this morning she was putting aside her differences and coming together tonight to celebrate Chill. All the kids were in the house doing arts and crafts with Renee. I told her to call my phone if the kids got too wild. Especially my niece and nephew Faith and LJ.

After about an hour of hosting the guest alone, Chill came in with Snoopy and Jack. Before we locked eyes, I was just staring at the finest man in the room. Everyone else was too, watching as he moved through the backyard. The man of the hour was mine and boy did he look good in his all-black outfit. When he got to me and I smelled that cologne, I melted into his arms as chocolate melts in a closed fist.

"Hey."

"Hi, Daddy."

"Mm, mm, mm." He sucked his teeth looking me up and down.

"You know you wearing the hell out of this dress tonight, right?" He hugged me from the back.

"You think so?"

"Hell yeah, I want a bite bad, but I'll wait until our guest leave."

"That's up to you babe, you know I'm a buffet open 24 hours for you."

"Seven days a week?"

"Seven." I smiled and laid a kiss on his lips. Jack and Snoopy then greeted me and Nick came up already tipsy slapping hands with them.

"Oh, yeah. All y'all niggas shinning and shit and matching and shit looking like some gangsta power rangers at the neck. I see how it is." He nodded his head in his feelings as Chill started to laugh.

"Don't cry, cry baby. You know I got my baby brother." Chill pulled out a long flat jeweler box from his waistband.

"Red for you, hot head mutha fucka." Chill handed him the box and he started smiling hard as hell.

"Damn, everybody got jewelry but baby mama. That's what's up." I joked, pinching Chill's cheek.

"Your jewelry is upstairs on the east wing. Come on, let's go get it now." He pulled me away from the crowd. We walked up the stairs and all the way across the house to the part I never really came to.

"Baby, why did you put something in a room way over here?" I asked as Chill opened the door. When we walked into the room, there was a trail of rose petals and candles going out to the terrace. A saxophonist was playing the most romantic music I ever heard and when I stepped out to the patio I was blown away by all red roses everywhere.

I turned around to speak to Chill and he was down on one knee with the most beautiful ring I ever saw out in front of me. I placed my hand over my mouth and started to cry so hard I couldn't breathe.

"Chill." Was all I could get out as he smiled and waited for me to catch my breath.

"Baby, are you serious? Is this for real?"

"Hell yeah, it is. Tish, when I met you, I had no idea how much you would change my life. Had I known you were my soulmate I wouldn't have spent a day without you. I've realized now that you are my soulmate, the missing piece that made me whole. Every day since we've reconnected, I've cherished every moment we've shared, and I don't want to spend a single day without you by my side. Your love has brought me so much joy, happiness, and fulfillment in my life. So, Tish?"

"Yes, baby?" Tears covered my entire face.

"Will you marry me?"

"Yes, yes baby. I will." I started to fan myself with my right hand as he slid the ring on my finger. Chill stood up from the ground and he picked me up into his arms as he spun me around. I can't believe I get to marry the man of my dreams, while having the perfect family, in the perfect house.

Now I feel like I can sit back, relax, and be on chill with my billionaire. No more drama, no more pain, just happiness.

The End

To keep up with new releases from Author Black Lavish join my readers group on Facebook

Author Black Lavish Books

Made in the USA
Middletown, DE
31 March 2024